"If Sar... ...and as a dowry."

Anger coursed through Wolf at Sarita's grandfather's statement. Wolf stood on one side of the old man, and his competition for the land—a smooth-talking lawyer—stood on the other. "Sarita's not going to take kindly to you 'buying' her a husband," Wolf said.

"Then I suggest we don't tell her," the old man said. "If either of you breathes a word of this to Sarita, I'll sell the land to whoever *didn't*."

"I'll keep the secret," the lawyer said. "I'd best be on my way, since I have some courting to do. Your granddaughter is a fine-looking woman," he added on his way out.

"If you want that land, Wolf, I suggest you go do some courting yourself," the old man said. "You have serious competition."

"I would never consider marrying a woman for a piece of land," Wolf said. "Besides, Sarita and I are natural-born antagonists."

The old man simply smiled.

Dear Reader,

Silhouette Romance novels aren't just for other women—the wonder of a Silhouette Romance is that it can touch *your* heart. And this month's selections are guaranteed to leave you smiling!

In Suzanne McMinn's engaging BUNDLES OF JOY title, *The Billionaire and the Bassinet,* a blue blood finds his hardened heart irrevocably tamed. This month's FABULOUS FATHERS offering by Jodi O'Donnell features an emotional, heartwarming twist you won't soon forget; in *Dr. Dad to the Rescue,* a man discovers strength and the healing power of love from one *very* special lady. *Marrying O'Malley,* the renegade who'd been her childhood nemesis, seemed the perfect way for a bride-to-be to thwart an unwanted betrothal—until their unlikely alliance stirred an even more incredible passion; don't miss this latest winner by Elizabeth August!

The Cowboy Proposes...Marriage? Get the charming lowdown as WRANGLERS & LACE continues with this sizzling story by Cathy Forsythe. Cara Colter will make you laugh and cry with *A Bride Worth Waiting For,* the story of the boy next door who *didn't* get the girl, but who'll stop at nothing to have her now. For readers who love powerful, dramatic stories, you won't want to miss *Paternity Lessons,* Maris Soule's uplifting FAMILY MATTERS tale.

Enjoy this month's titles—and please drop me a line about *why* you keep coming back to Romance. I want to make sure we continue fulfilling *your* dreams!

Regards,

Mary-Theresa Hussey

Mary-Theresa Hussey
Senior Editor Silhouette Romance

Please address questions and book requests to:
Silhouette Reader Service
U.S.: 3010 Walden Ave., P.O. Box 1325, Buffalo, NY 14269
Canadian: P.O. Box 609, Fort Erie, Ont. L2A 5X3

MARRYING O'MALLEY

Elizabeth August

Silhouette
R O M A N C E™
Published by Silhouette Books
America's Publisher of Contemporary Romance

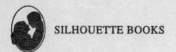

SILHOUETTE BOOKS

ISBN 0-373-19386-6

MARRYING O'MALLEY

Visit us at www.romance.net

Printed in U.S.A.

Books by Elizabeth August

ELIZABETH AUGUST

lives in the mountains of North Carolina with her husband, Doug, a chemist. They have three grown sons. Their oldest is pursuing a career in medicine, their middle son is a chemical engineer and their youngest is now in college.

Having survived a bout with cancer, Elizabeth has now joined the ranks of cancer survivors. Writing will always be her primary pursuit and will remain at the top of her list of loves just below her husband, sons and daughter-in-law.

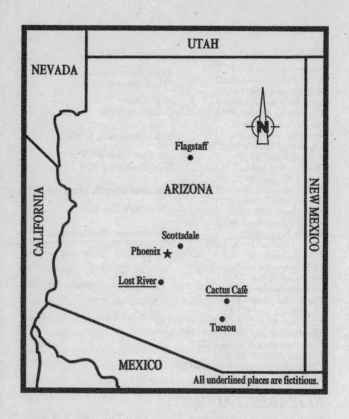

UTAH

NEVADA

ARIZONA

CALIFORNIA

NEW MEXICO

Flagstaff

Scottsdale

Phoenix ★

Lost River ●

Cactus Café
●

Tucson

MEXICO

All underlined places are fictitious.

Chapter One

Returning to Lost River had not been in Wolf O'Malley's plans. But a couple of days ago he'd learned of his father's death nearly two months earlier. The news had come as a shock, but he hadn't returned to pay his last respects to his father. He'd come out of respect to his mother's memory and to claim what should rightfully be his. He wanted nothing that had belonged to the O'Malleys; it was the dowry that his mother had taken into her marriage, land that had belonged to her family for generations, that he'd come for. Willow O'Malley had died when he was ten, but time had not dulled his memories of her. Her spirit, he knew, would not rest easy with her land in the hands of Katherine O'Malley, Frank's second wife.

He had sent no word of his arrival ahead. Surprise was always an advantage, and where Katherine was concerned, a man would be a fool not to use any advantage in his favor. Last night he'd stayed in Phoenix, intending to make his presence first known when he walked into Bradford Dillion's law office at nine this morning. But a mixture of emotions had refused to allow him to rest. He'd risen before dawn, and now, as the first rays of light were barely peeking over the horizon, he sought out his father's grave.

The O'Malley plot, the burial site of four generations of his father's family, loomed ahead of him, enclosed by a low iron fence. Standing in front of one of the graves was a woman. Her thick black hair was plaited into a single braid that hung nearly to her waist, and she was clothed in faded jeans, a blue blouse and sneakers.

Changing direction slightly, he used a nearby tree to mask his approach until he could get a look at her face. Pretty, of Mexican descent, he noted. His gaze narrowed as recognition dawned. She'd matured, lost that girlish, impish look, but he knew without a doubt that the woman was Sarita Lopez. So what was she doing at his family plot? The last he recalled, she had no connection to anyone in his family. While he watched, she bowed her head and clasped her hands together, presumably saying a prayer.

Leaving the shadow of the tree, he continued to the plot, stepping over the low fence instead of entering through the break left for visitors.

Sarita straightened abruptly as a flash of boot caught her eye. No one ever came to the cemetery this early. Silently she cursed under her breath. The last thing in the world she wanted was for anyone to find out she paid visits to the O'Malley plot.

Frantically trying to think of some plausible excuse, she met the intruder's gaze. At first her mind refused to comprehend what she saw. The facial features of the tall, muscular man standing in front of her were harsher than she remembered, but there was no mistaking his identity. The color drained from her face. As her knees threatened to buckle, two strong hands closed around her upper arms.

"I never thought of you as the fainting type," Wolf said.

"I thought you were dead!" she exclaimed. For one brief moment she considered the possibility that her imagination was working overtime. But her imagination wasn't that good. Through the fabric of her shirt she could feel the calluses on his palms and the heat radiating from his hands was as hot as the flame of a log.

Startled by this statement, Wolf looked at the gravestone in front of where she'd placed the flower. It bore his name. According to the inscription, he'd been dead for six years. A bitter taste filled his mouth as the anger he'd thought he'd conquered returned. Seeing her color returning, he released her. "Did my father even send out a search party?"

The cold, icy glint in his eyes and the hard, authoritative set of his jaw were all as she remembered. Still, Sarita was finding it difficult to believe he was really there. "The wreckage of the plane you were in was found on a mountainside. It took the Canadian authorities two weeks to get a rescue team to the site. They found the remains of two bodies. From what I gather there wasn't much left to identify. The plane had burned on impact. Since you and the pilot were the only scheduled people onboard, it was assumed the bodies belonged to the two of you."

"A backwoodsman, a friend of the pilot, showed up at the last minute and we agreed to give him a lift back to his place. It was on our way. Apparently the pilot must not have taken the time to add the man's name to his passenger list, and no one else must have noticed the man coming onboard.''

"Apparently," Sarita replied. "But how did you get out of the plane? The authorities said it was a terrible impact."

"My seat belt must have been defective. It opened. I was thrown forward, my head hit something hard, and the world went black. I figure I went through the front windshield. Anyway, when I regained consciousness, I was in a snowbank about thirty feet from the charred wreckage in pretty bad shape but alive." The bitterness in his voice deepened. "Guess nobody was all that interested in questioning the identity of the bodies. My being dead was as good a resolution to the conflicts between me and my father as any."

Everyone in town knew Wolf had left because of the bitter feelings between him and his dad. It was possible he wouldn't care, but she thought he deserved to know that his death had affected his father strongly. "I'm sure he didn't feel that way. I take the shortcut through the cemetery almost daily and say a prayer over my parents' and my grandmother's graves on my way into town. Many mornings I saw him here. On your birthday he'd bring a special token…a feather or stone. The pain I saw on his face convinced me he regretted that things were never set right between the two of you."

Knowing his father had felt some remorse caused a momentary chink in Wolf's armor of cynicism, but flashes of memory quickly mended the dent. "His regrets came a little too late."

She was still finding this turn of events hard to comprehend. "How did you survive? Where have you

been? Why didn't you come back?'' She blurted out
the questions in quick succession.

"An old woodsman found me and nursed me to back
to health. For the first time since my mother's death I
found peace there with him in the wilderness. And
since no one had come looking for me, I figured no
one would miss me, so I stayed.'' His gaze returned to
her, and the question that had entered his mind when
he first saw her repeated itself. "I am curious as to
why you're here. We were never on good terms.''

She'd asked herself that same thing many times and
had not been able to come up with an answer. There
was no reason his death should have affected her as
deeply as it had. Her pride refused to let him guess that
she'd missed him, so she shrugged to indicate her actions were of little consequence. "With your father
gone, I figured someone should remember you.'' Not
wanting to give him a chance to question her further,
she strode away.

Wolf watched her leave. She was right about there
possibly being no one left to mourn him. Katherine, his
stepmother, had taught him to distrust and had turned
him bitter toward the world. By the time he'd left to
inspect his father's interests in Alaska, he'd alienated
a great many people.

In his mind's eye he saw Joe Johnson, the old
woodsman who had found him. "Anger muddles the
mind and dulls the senses,'' Joe had cautioned him
many times. "You become the prey instead of the
hunter.''

Wolf turned back to his father's gravestone. He had
not been entirely honest with Sarita. Grudgingly he admitted to himself that at least part of the reason he'd
stayed in the wilderness with Joe was because he was

hiding out, escaping the constant battles with his step-mother. "I will not be bested a second time by that she-devil you married," he vowed, his emotions once again under stern control.

When the prickling on the back of her neck ceased, Sarita glanced over her shoulder to see Wolf again staring at his father's stone. A smile began to curl one corner of her mouth. She wanted to issue a shriek of delight. He was alive! It was as if a rush of fresh, sweet air was swirling around her, giving the day a sense of energy and renewal.

In the next instant the smile had turned to a self-directed scowl. It didn't make any sense that his being alive should mean that much to her. They were the same age and had both grown up in this town. And from the beginning she and Wolf O'Malley had been at odds with each other. A flush of embarrassment red-dened her neck and traveled upward. He was probably thinking she was a desperately lonely woman to waste her time stopping by the grave of a man who had not even been a friend.

And she couldn't blame him if he did think that. There had been many times when she'd considered cutting those visits from her morning route. But she hadn't. She pondered this as she continued into town.

"You look like you've seen a ghost," Gladys Ko-waski, Sarita's fellow waitress said, looking up from giving the tables a final inspection as Sarita entered the Cactus Café. The thirty-two-year-old, pretty, blond, blue-eyed woman gave her body a shake to imitate an exaggerated chill. "I don't know how you can walk through that cemetery every morning. It gives me the creeps."

"The unhappy souls haunt the places where they died, not their graves." Sarita tossed back her usual rebuttal, unable to recall how many times she and Gladys had had this same exchange.

Gladys continued to regard her narrowly. "No, really. This morning you look as if something really shook you."

Sarita wasn't ready to discuss Wolf O'Malley. Besides, it occurred to her that maybe he wasn't ready for anyone to know he was in town. He had chosen a very early hour to visit the cemetery. "There's just something unusual in the air, don't you think?" she replied, continuing into the back room to find her apron.

"And what has my two lovely waitresses looking as if they are on the verge of an argument this morning?" Jules Desmond, the owner and chef, asked as the two women entered the kitchen where he was preparing the food for cooking and serving. He added a "tisk-tisk." "Strife is not good for the customers' digestion."

"And neither is your food with all those chilies you put in it," Gladys returned.

Jules, fifty-eight, widowed, balding and slightly on the plump side, skewed his face into an exaggerated expression of dismay. "That was an unfair cut."

Looking repentant, Gladys put her arm around his shoulders. "You're right. Your cooking is actually very good."

Jules's smile returned. "So what's going on between the two of you?"

"Nothing," Sarita assured him.

Disappointment showed on his face. "In New York there was always some juicy gossip to start the day, or at least one dispute between the employees that needed settling. Here there is next to nothing."

"Your doctor sent you here for your health. You're supposed to be living in a relaxed, laid-back environment," Gladys reminded him.

He tossed her a disgruntled look. "I would like a little more excitement than wondering if Charlie Gregor will order his omelet with pickles or without today."

"Maybe you'll get it. Sarita says she can feel something unusual in the air."

Jules turned his attention to Sarita. "You could be right. Mary Beth came in last night to bake pies, and not only did she bake her usuals, she made a gooseberry one, a chocolate layer cake and a coconut layer cake."

"Sounds more like she's pregnant again," Gladys said. "Or she had a hell of a fight with Ned. Both send her into cooking frenzies."

A knock on the front door caused them all to look through the serving slit to the public area of the café.

"Looks like Charlie's here," Jules said, glancing at the clock over the stove. "And right on the minute. Time to open up."

"Fifty cents he wants pickles this morning," Gladys wagered, heading out of the kitchen.

"No bet," Sarita replied. "This morning I wouldn't be surprised if he wanted sauerkraut."

Gladys glanced back at her. "You really meant it when you said you thought there was something unusual in the air."

"Believe me, today this town could be in for a surprise," Sarita replied.

Gladys stopped, the expression on her face stern. "What...?"

Charlie knocked harder on the door and Sarita

wished she'd kept her mouth shut. She wasn't a gossip. When Wolf O'Malley wanted people to know he was in town, he'd let them know. "Better get that door open before Charlie breaks it down."

Realizing she wasn't going to get any answer that would satisfy her, Gladys grinned good-naturedly. "Now that would be news. Starving Patron Breaks Down Door of Local Diner to Get to Food. We'd probably have people coming all the way from Phoenix for breakfast," she jested, hurrying to open the door.

"'Bout time," Charlie grumbled, shuffling in and taking a seat at his usual table by the window. Tall and only slightly stooped with age, lanky, with skin deeply wrinkled, permanently tanned and leathery from a lifetime spent in the outdoors, at ninety-seven years of age, he was the oldest resident of their town and some thought the most cantankerous. "There's a chill in the air today," he announced. "I'll have black coffee, scrambled eggs, bacon and a side of beans and biscuits."

"You're right. There's definitely something in the air. Charlie didn't even order an omelet," Gladys said as she passed Sarita on her way to the kitchen.

During the next few minutes the usual early-morning customers began to come in. The sheriff and a couple of his deputies joined the mayor for their regular off-the-record meeting to discuss issues important to them or relay any important information about happenings during the night.

Bradford Dillion took his usual seat toward the back. Elderly, lanky and dressed in a three-piece suit, he'd been the O'Malley family lawyer for as long as anyone could remember. Sarita trusted and liked him and was grateful his table was in her section.

She was equally grateful that Greg Pike's table wasn't. He, too, was a lawyer. In his late forties, handsome and always well dressed, he was considered quite a catch by many in town. But he was too glib for her taste. He always had something flattering to say, but to her it didn't ring true. As usual he was joined by Henry Jarrot, the president of the Lost River Bank and Frank O'Malley's former business partner.

"Sarita." Greg Pike waved her over.

She knew what he wanted and she might as well get it out of the way early. "What can I do for you, Mr. Pike?" she asked, approaching his table.

"Your granddaddy ready to sell that worthless land of his yet?" Greg asked.

"He doesn't consider it worthless. He considers it my legacy."

"We're offering him more than fair market value. There's nobody else who's even going to want it. If I was you, I'd talk to him. You two can keep the house and an acre, maybe even two or four, surrounding it. He'll still have his home and his garden and he won't have to tend other people's yards or weed their gardens to made ends meet. As for you, you'll have a nice nest egg in the bank."

"We make ends meet just fine. He takes the yard and gardening jobs because he likes to keep busy. Like I've told you, the land is a part of who he is." She eyed him suspiciously. Ever since he'd made the offer for the seventy acres her grandfather owned, she'd wondered why. "Besides, I don't understand what's so important about my grandfather's land. There's plenty of other property you could buy for less."

"Now that Katherine…Mrs. O'Malley owns the land adjacent to his, she's considering building a health spa…a place where the wealthy from Phoenix can come and be rejuvenated,'' Greg Pike elaborated. "She wants to ensure her guests privacy by having plenty of land surrounding the main buildings, plus she wants to provide them with an expanse for horseback riding. But most important, she feels that spring in the canyon on your grandfather's property would be the perfect draw…an oasis in the midst of this arid land.''

"Paul Glasgow tried that spa idea and went bankrupt.''

"But he didn't have a picturesque spring to p—'' Greg's protest died in his throat. His jaw froze and Sarita noticed Henry Jarrot pale, then realized that the entire diner had suddenly become quiet. Everyone was staring at the door. Even before she turned to see who had come in, she knew.

"Well, I'll be damned,'' Charlie chortled. "Talk about rising from the dead.''

"It can't be,'' Henry Jarrot muttered, his tone telling Sarita he was not happy about this turn of events.

"Wolf? Wolf O'Malley?'' Bradford Dillion had risen and was heading toward the newcomer, his hand outstretched. "Is it really you?''

"In the flesh,'' Wolf replied. He'd been standing in the doorway, his bulk nearly filling it. Now he strode to meet the elderly lawyer. Figuring Sarita had already spread the word about his arrival, he'd decided that keeping in the shadows before he went to Bradford's office was a waste of his time. But from the expressions on everyone's faces, he guessed he'd misjudged her. Clearly she hadn't said anything to anyone about him. "I was just going to have some breakfast before coming to see you.''

"Join me, boy, join me. You're a sight for sore

eyes." Bradford had reached him and combined a welcoming handshake with a one-armed hug.

"Katherine O'Malley ain't going to like this," the sheriff drawled in hushed tones that carried to the others at his table and a few nearby including Sarita. She saw the mayor and deputies nod.

"You're going to have to say something to him," Greg insisted to Henry. Suspicion entered his voice. "Make sure it's really him."

Out of the corner of her eye, Sarita saw the facade of friendliness spread over Henry's face.

"Wolf. Returned from the dead. What a surprise," Henry said, rising and moving toward the two men heading to Bradford's table.

Wolf stopped and turned to his father's former business partner. "Henry." He extended his hand.

Henry accepted the handshake and added a pat to Wolf's shoulder. "Give me a call when you're ready to discuss the business."

Wolf raised a questioning eyebrow.

"Your father never changed his will," Bradford said. "Katherine got the house, a healthy chunk of cash and all the personal belongings, but the rest, including the business, was divided equally between her, you, your half sister and your stepbrother."

Wolf's gaze swung to him. "My mother's land."

"All yours," Bradford assured him.

Wolf breathed a satisfied sigh.

Sarita, who had taken a step back, saw Greg's hand tighten into a fist around his napkin. He definitely didn't like this turn of events. It was Wolf's mother's land that was adjacent to Sarita's grandfather's...the land Katherine had earmarked for her spa. That Greg hadn't raced out the door to contact Katherine

O'Malley showed a certain amount of reserve, Sarita thought. Then she realized that he wouldn't want to leave until he'd found out all he could.

Still embarrassed that Wolf had found her at his grave site, she would have preferred to remain in the background. But that would be cowardly, and pride refused to allow her to exhibit cowardliness in front of him. As Henry Jarrot returned to his table, she approached Bradford's table. "Would you like something to drink while you decide what you want for breakfast?" she addressed Wolf in cool, efficient tones.

He looked up at her. Sarita Lopez had never behaved like he'd expected her to. "Apparently you are very good at keeping secrets," he said in hushed tones.

"I figured that when you wanted people to know you were back, you'd let them know yourself," she replied.

He nodded his approval. "I appreciate that."

Glad she'd followed her instincts, Sarita noted that this had to be the first time the two of them hadn't been arguing by the second sentence.

"You knew he was in town?" Bradford asked in the same lowered voice.

"I wanted to pay my respects to my mother," Wolf elaborated. "We bumped into each other at the cemetery. She thought she was seeing a ghost."

Grateful he hadn't mentioned that she was at his grave site, she caught the look in his eye that told her he considered them even. And that suited her just fine. Returning her attention to her reason for even approaching him, she repeated, "Would you like something to drink while you look over the menu or are you ready to order?"

He glanced down at the menu. "Coffee to drink and

I'll have the Cowhand's Special. Scramble the eggs,'' he replied.

"Coming up." Walking away, she saw the rest of the customers casting covert glances in Wolf's direction. And unlike normal mornings when conversations flooded the place, voices overlapping each other until they were a muddle of noise, this morning conversations were being held softly, confining what was said to the occupants of the individual tables.

As she laid the paper containing Wolf's order on the high, metal counter of the window between the kitchen and the serving area, Jules motioned her inside. Knowing she was going to have to talk to him sooner or later, she entered the kitchen.

"Who is this Wolf O'Malley?" he demanded in lowered tones, trying to keep an eye on his cooking food while watching for any further activity among the customers. "This is the first real excitement I've seen in this town since Norma Alexander caught Rupert Gordon peeping in her bedroom window."

"He's Frank O'Malley's eldest son. Everyone thought he was dead," Sarita replied. "Now I've really got to get back to my customers."

But before she could make her escape, Gladys entered. "Isn't this the most exciting thing? Ms. High and Mighty Katherine O'Malley is not going to like it."

Jules looked confused. "I'd think she would be glad her son was alive."

"He's not her son," Gladys explained. "He's her stepson. His mother was Willow Bluefeather."

"An Indian?" Jules asked, his interest increasing.

Gladys nodded. "Full-blooded Cherokee. I don't remember her well. I do remember that she was very pretty."

Jules peered harder out the window. "Yes, he does look as if he has Native American blood in him."

"Willow Bluefeather O'Malley was beautiful and one of the sweetest women in the world," Sarita said, recalling the kindness Willow had always exhibited toward everyone. "She died of some complication associated with the flu when Wolf was ten. His father married Katherine when he was twelve. He and his stepmother never got along."

A knowing look came over Gladys's face. "My Roy has always said Katherine wanted Wolf out of the picture so her own children could inherit everything." In response to Jules's raised eyebrow, she added, "Preston O'Malley was her son from a previous marriage. She made sure Frank adopted him so he would be sure to share in the inheritance. Claudia is Frank and Katherine's child, but I think she only had her to satisfy Frank. Anyone can see that Katherine is partial to Preston. She thinks the sun rises and sets on him."

Jules nodded his head. "She's definitely spoiled him."

Sarita had only been half listening. She'd been recalling how badly Wolf had taken his mother's passing. In spite of the fact that she and he had never gotten along, she'd felt obliged to seek him out and offer her condolences. He'd growled at her, and she'd never approached him again. And she didn't like gossiping about him now. She nodded toward the bacon that was fast becoming too crisp to serve. "We'd better get back to our customers, and you'd better get back to your cooking," she told Jules.

Letting out a cry of dismay, he quickly returned his attention to his stove.

"Looks like life is going to get real interesting around here for a while," Gladys noted as she and Sarita left the kitchen.

"I suppose *interesting* is as good a word as any," Sarita muttered back, doubting Katherine O'Malley would use that same adjective.

Chapter Two

Sarita looked at the clock. It was nearly three. The normal hours for the diner were from 7 a.m. to 2 p.m. Constantly reminding people that he was semiretired, Jules reserved the rest of the day to work on recipes for the cookbook he was creating or pursuing his second passion...golf. Normally the last of their customers cleared out by two-thirty. Today the place was still half-full. And Jules wasn't helping to ease the customers out, either. He'd closed down the kitchen and come out front, but instead of subtly mentioning that the afternoon was getting late, he was pouring coffee and entering into the various conversations about Wolf's return from the grave.

The general consensus was that Katherine would be furious and she was a dangerous woman when riled.

"But Wolf O'Malley can be just as dangerous. Even more so," Vivian Kale said, loud enough for all to hear.

Several others nodded knowingly.

Sarita knew what they were thinking. Her sense of fairness refused to let her remain silent. "There was never any proof those rumors were true."

"What rumors?" Jules demanded.

"Some people think he pushed Katherine down the stairs when he was fifteen. Broke her arm," one of the men said.

"The story she told was that she fell on her own," Sarita reminded them all.

"Yeah, but her telling that tale never rang true to my ears. Could be she said it to keep peace in the family and the police out of it," Vivian argued. "And, as I recall, Frank shipped Wolf off to that military academy right afterward."

"Because his highfalutin stepmom had been trying to get rid of Wolf all along. Wouldn't put it past her to have faked that fall down the stairs." Charlie entered the fray. He didn't usually come back for lunch, but Sarita had noted that several who only came for breakfast had come a second time today. And she was grateful Charlie was there. It was only right that Wolf should have at least one customer who would stick up for him.

"Her broken arm was no fake," Vivian retorted.

"Could be she didn't plan on breaking it," Charlie rebutted.

"You've never liked Katherine O'Malley," Vivian fumed. "You'd take Wolf's side if you'd seen him doing the deed."

Charlie glared at her. "Wouldn't lie for no man nor woman."

"Now, now. Keep your tempers under control," Jules soothed.

One of the men laughed. "This ain't nothing compared to what's probably going on at the O'Malley place right now.''

The rest nodded, almost in unison.

''My money's on Katherine,'' another customer called out from a side table.

''You weren't around when Wolf came back to town after college,'' another spoke up. ''Never seen a man so cold or in control.''

''Looks like six years away hasn't changed him, either,'' Vivian said. ''When I passed him on the street a little bit ago, he gave me an icy stare that sent chills down my spine.''

Vivian, Sarita noted, was really getting on her nerves. ''He's probably had people staring at him all day. He was just returning tit for tat.''

Vivian snorted. ''I don't know why you're so intent on defending him. I don't recall the two of you being such good friends.''

Sarita was surprised herself by the intensity of her desire to defend Wolf. It was very close to a need. ''We weren't, but I don't think it's right to sit here and condemn him with unsubstantiated gossip.''

''Bradford Dillion obviously likes him,'' Jules pointed out. ''I've always thought he was a good judge of character.''

''Bradford Dillion was a friend of Wolf's mother and her family. I don't think he ever approved of Frank's marriage to Katherine,'' Vivian said.

Sarita found herself fighting the urge to shove a pie into the woman's face. Shocked that she would consider going to such lengths on Wolf's behalf, she reminded herself that Vivian had always gotten on her nerves.

''And the fact that Katherine has made it clear she

intends to petition the court to have Dillion removed as executor of Frank's estate and Greg Pike put in his place might have something to do with Dillion's joy at seeing Wolf. Wolf will fight her tooth and nail to see that his father's wishes are followed to the letter, especially any that go against hers," one of the men from the back offered.

"If I were Katherine O'Malley, I'd hire a bodyguard." Vivian gave her head a violent nod to add emphasis to her words.

Sarita's patience came within a hair of snapping. "That's the most absurd thing I've ever heard." When only Charlie added a grunt of support, it did snap. She glared at the assembly. "Don't you all have something better to do with your afternoon than sit around and rehash old gossip?"

Jules looked at her worriedly, then a look of apology spread over his face as his gaze swept his customers. "It is past three."

In a mild flurry of activity, the patrons paid and left.

When he, Gladys and Sarita were alone, Sarita braced herself to be fired. Instead Jules studied her with interest. "I've never seen you lose your temper. Is Wolf O'Malley an old flame that hasn't quite died?"

"I didn't know you even knew him," Gladys muttered, also studying Sarita. "The two of you didn't act like old friends when he was in here this morning."

"When he was still going to school here, we were in the same class. And, you're right, we weren't friends. But I felt someone should stick up for him. It was like a lynch mob in here." Not wanting to answer any more questions, she looked to Jules and said stiffly, "Now are you going to fire me or shall we get this place cleaned up so we can go home?"

"It's been a long day. Let's clean up this place," he replied.

Both Gladys and Jules allowed her to do her work in peace, but she could feel them covertly looking her way every once in a while and was glad when she was finally on her way home.

The old rambling adobe ranch house she shared with her grandfather was a couple of miles out of town. In bad weather she drove. In good weather she preferred to walk. As she neared the end of the long, dirt driveway, she could see Luis Lopez seated, as usual, in his cane chair on the front porch, whittling. The chair was balanced on the two back legs, and his feet were propped up on the porch railing.

"*Abuelo,* did you hear the news?" she asked, mounting the porch, then leaning against one of the pillars holding up the roof.

He grinned, causing the deep weather-induced wrinkles of his permanently tanned skin to become even more pronounced. "If you're talking about Wolf O'Malley returning, I did. I was weeding Mrs. Yager's flower garden when the young Ballori woman came by to tell her. Seems his reappearance has caused quite a stir."

Sarita nodded. "This turn of events should stop Greg Pike from pestering us about purchasing this land."

"You'd think so." Luis's grin disappeared. "But it hasn't. When I came home for lunch, he was on our doorstep with an even bigger offer. He says that since we have the spring on our property, Katherine can still build her spa."

"Once she gets a notion, she's like a dog with a bone," Sarita muttered.

"I've been thinking that maybe I should sell."

Shock registered on Sarita's face. "You can't be serious. You love this land."

"I'm an old man. I'm satisfied with my life. But you…you could take the money to travel, to see the world."

Sarita saw the worry in his eyes and guessed what was really on his mind. "I like it here. This land is as much a part of me as it is of you. It's where I belong. And if I want to see the world, I've got enough saved up to take a trip."

"You could go to college."

They'd had this discussion before, as well. "I don't want to go to college. I like my life as it is."

"You have taken the vow you made to your father to watch over me much too seriously. You've restricted your opportunities. You work at the café, you come home and work in the garden, you ride your horse, you take care of me. What kind of life is that?"

"Peaceful." Silently she admitted that there were times when her life seemed to lack fulfillment, but she wasn't ready to admit that to her grandfather. Both her mother and grandmother had died when she was very young. Her father and grandfather had raised her. When she was in her late teens her father had died, leaving her the only one left to watch over the old man in front of her, and she would not shirk that duty.

"I worry about what will happen to you when I'm gone. I don't want to see you alone in the world. You should have a husband and a family."

They'd had this conversation a hundred times before. Her usual response was to say that she would do just fine on her own, that she liked being an independent woman. The words formed on the tip of her tongue, but when she opened her mouth, she heard herself saying, "All right. I'll admit, I'd like to find a husband and have a family. But I'm not so desperate I'd take your money and go scouring the world or college campuses for one."

Triumph glistened in his eyes. "You could go stay with my cousin José in Mexico City," he coaxed. "The last time you were there, you had four proposals."

"They wanted an American wife so they could come to this country."

"You don't have enough faith in yourself. One, maybe two, had that in mind, but not all four. I know for a fact that Greco was in love with you."

"He got over it fast enough. He was married within two months of the time I left and the father of twins barely nine months later."

"You rejected him and he was forced to move on with his life."

"For someone as desperately in love as he claimed, he moved on fairly quickly, don't you think?" she returned dryly.

Luis's gaze narrowed on her with purpose. "I want to see you married, with a husband to look after you."

"I don't *need* anyone to look after me." She gave an impatient snort. "Men! If I was a male you wouldn't be so anxious about my being married."

"You're wrong. I would want you to have a wife to look after you. When the Lord ordered Noah to gather all the animals in pairs, he did it for a reason. The man looks after the woman and the woman looks after the man. Together they make a whole."

"I feel perfectly whole on my own."

"Evening," a male voice drawled, as its owner rounded the corner of the house.

Startled, Sarita gasped.

"Guess I forgot to mention that Wolf is going to be boarding with us," her grandfather said.

"I was driving by your place to take a look at my property when I saw the Room for Rent sign," Wolf said, mounting the porch.

Sarita stared at him. "You and me under the same roof?"

"I know we used to get on each other nerves as kids but we're adults now. I figure we can keep our tempers in check."

"Sure, no problem." She knew she'd sound childish if she voiced any doubts, but already the thought of his continued presence was causing an uneasiness within. *He's right, grow up,* she ordered herself.

"I told him he could have kitchen privileges as long as he cleans up after himself. And he's paying extra to have his evening meal provided," Luis spoke up. "I warned him it wouldn't be anything fancy. I've got a stew cooking for tonight. Figured you could make some corn bread."

"Corn bread, sure," she managed levelly.

Wolf nodded his approval. "Stew and corn bread sound great."

Getting over the shock of seeing him, Sarita began to wonder how much of the conversation between her grandfather and her he'd overheard. Voices traveled on the arid air. Her shoulders stiffened with pride. So what if he knew she was on her way to spinsterhood? Even if he hadn't overheard, he'd have guessed it soon enough. He knew she was twenty-eight. And it was obvious she wasn't married. If he stuck around, he'd soon learn she didn't have any prospects, either. "I'll go check on the stew."

After giving the stew a quick stir, Sarita could not

keep herself from doing a little eavesdropping at the living room window. Wolf had settled into the chair beside her grandfather on the front porch, and the men were discussing the weather and whether it would be a hard winter or not. Self-mockery spread over her face as she admitted to herself that she'd been afraid they'd been discussing her. *You're the last subject in the world that would interest Wolf O'Malley,* her inner voice chided.

Leaving the men on their own, she busied herself in the guest room, making certain it was dusted and fresh linens were on the bed. A single leather satchel lay on the floor, still packed. Staring down at it, she recalled that once during her teenage years she'd found herself unexpectedly attracted to him and visualized him suddenly looking her way, seeing her as appealing and coming to call.

"Now that was a moment of lunacy," she grumbled to herself. Scowling at the bag, she hoped he would change his mind and seek other quarters.

"There's nothing in there that will bite."

Jerking her gaze to the door, she saw Wolf standing there, watching her from behind a shuttered mask. "I was just getting your room into shape," she managed evenly.

He continued to stand in the doorway, blocking her escape. "If you're worried that I'll harm you or your grandfather, I promise you I won't."

She frowned in confusion. "That thought never crossed my mind."

He scowled with disbelief. "I know the stories Katherine spread about me. Everyone in town thinks I pushed her down those stairs."

"Not everyone. I never did. And neither did my father or grandfather."

His expression remained skeptical.

Feeling the need to prove her words, she added, "It's not that we didn't think she could have provoked you into it, it's just that if you had done it, you would have admitted it."

Bitterness etched itself into his features. "It's a shame my father didn't have the same faith in me."

"From what I've heard, Katherine can be very persuasive."

Purpose replaced the bitterness on his face. "This time she'll learn that she's met her match."

Sarita suddenly was worried for him. She'd seen Katherine in action and knew the woman could be a formidable foe. "Be careful," she warned.

"I plan to," Wolf assured her.

She found herself considering offering her aid, should he need it, and recalled the last time she'd tried to befriend him. No sense in embarrassing herself a second time, she decided. "I should get back to the kitchen." Edging toward the door, she gave him space to move out of her way.

Stepping aside, Wolf let her pass. As she headed down the hall, he watched her. Earlier in the day, Bradford had offered him a room at his place and he'd accepted. But when he'd driven out to the land that had brought him back, he'd passed the Lopez property and seen the Room for Rent sign on their gate. His curiosity still piqued by his early-morning encounter with Sarita at the cemetery, he'd called Bradford and told him that his plans had changed.

He frowned as he started to unpack. Sarita Lopez wasn't pleased to have him there. That was obvious.

So why the visit to his grave? Her explanation that she thought someone should remember him seemed lame considering their history. "Joe always said trying to read a woman's mind is harder than figuring reasons for God to have created mosquitoes," Wolf muttered under his breath. "And he's right."

His expression turned grim. "Except where my stepmother is concerned." He understood her very well. She was spoiled and selfish and would use any means to achieve her aims.

He smiled to himself as he put his clothes in the bureau. He'd come prepared to fight for the land that was his. Now there would be no need. Not only did he have the land, but a chunk of his father's wealth would be his along with a percentage of the family business. And he planned to make his presence felt.

The slamming of a car door caught his attention.

"Where is he?" a familiar female voice demanded.

Wolf strode down the hall, halting a few feet from the front door as Katherine pushed open the screen door and entered. "So you are alive." Her gaze raked over him. "I was in Houston when Greg called to tell me the news. I had to come see for myself."

"Greg Pike?" Wolf spoke in an easy drawl, keeping his posture relaxed as if her presence was of little concern. "Bradford did tell me you'd hired him to be your lawyer. Bradford said you even tried to have him removed as executor of my father's will and Pike put in his place."

Fury flashed in Katherine's eyes. "Bradford Dillion was your father's lawyer. He has never had my best interests at heart."

"Bradford Dillion is an honorable man."

Katherine shrugged as if that meant nothing to her,

then her expression turned icy. "I didn't come here to discuss Bradford Dillion. How much is it going to cost me to get you out of my life?"

"I'm planning on staying. My roots are here."

Katherine's cheeks flushed with rage. Issuing a snort of disgust, she pivoted and strode out of the house, ignoring both Sarita standing in the living room doorway and Luis who had risen and followed in Katherine's wake to the screened door.

"So you're gonna build yourself a home on Willow's land?" Luis asked as Katherine's car sped away.

Wolf shrugged. "Haven't decided what I'm going to do yet. But there's no reason for Katherine to know that."

Sarita eased back into the living room out of view of the men and drew a long, calming breath. She had tensed during the confrontation between Katherine and Wolf, her body readying itself to intercede if Katherine tried to harm him. Shaken by the strength of this unexpected instinct to protect him, she continued into the kitchen and sank into a chair at the table. Get a grip, she told herself. Wolf O'Malley was the last person in the world who needed or wanted her protection.

"I apologize for that scene just now."

Sarita jerked around to see Wolf crossing to the sink. The kitchen was the largest room in the house and had always seemed spacious to her until this moment. His presence suddenly made it seem small and crowded. Not wanting him to guess he was the reason she was so shaken, she said, "Your stepmother has always scared me a little."

"She's always scared me, too," he admitted with a crooked grin.

The unexpected boyishness on his face caused a curious curl within her.

"Glasses?" He motioned toward the cabinets.

"The one to your right." Remembering her manners, she added quickly, "Would you like some iced tea or soda?"

"Just water." Running a glassful, he drank half, then leaning against the counter, studied her thoughtfully. "The way I remember it, you and I didn't get along very well from day one."

Her gaze rested on his well-worn boots as her mind flashed back to their childhood. About a mile and a half farther down the road that ran in front of her grandfather's home, Frank O'Malley had built Willow O'Malley stables and corrals on the property that had been Willow's dowry so that she could keep horses and ride her land when she pleased. Even before he could walk, Willow would bring her son out to ride with her.

Frank O'Malley had hired Luis to caretake the stables and corrals and tend the horses. When Sarita was barely five, Luis began taking her along with him, thus hers and Wolf's paths had crossed very early. She raised her gaze to his face. "You were always trying to boss me around."

"You were always doing something that could get you hurt."

The same reproving tone he'd used when they were both seven years old laced his words and, as they had those many years ago, her eyes flashed with defiance. "We had a couple of horses, and I had my own pony. My grandfather had taught me all about taking care of them. I knew what I was doing."

Wolf remembered the small, dark-haired girl who had glared at him just as the woman she had become

was glaring at him now. "Guess we still know how to
get on each other's nerves."

"Seems that way," she admitted.

Another memory of their distant past returned. "You
still owe me a thank-you," he said.

Sarita knew what he was talking about. They'd been
fourteen at the time. She'd been out riding alone and
her horse had been spooked by a snake and thrown her.
When the horse came back to the barn alone, her grandfather had organized a search. It had been Wolf who
had found her. Despite their combative association,
she'd experienced a tingle of excitement that he'd been
her rescuer. Then he'd spoiled everything. "Enduring
a half hour lecture from you in that know-it-all tone of
yours killed any gratitude I was feeling."

Wolf recalled her sitting on a rock, her shirt torn and
leg bloodied. He'd hated seeing her injured. Even today
the memory bothered him. "You shouldn't have gone
out riding alone."

The hairs on the back of her neck bristled. "I was
old enough not to need a chaperon."

"Obviously you weren't."

"We were the same age, and you thought you were
old enough to go riding alone," she snapped.

Wolf eased himself away from the counter. "Looks
like we still mix like oil and water." Striding to the
door, he paused and looked back. "Thought maybe you
were stopping by my grave because you felt bad about
our fighting all the time. Guess I was wrong. Seems
that's part of our nature."

As his footfalls echoed down the hall, Sarita fought
the urge to scream. No one could rile her the way Wolf
O'Malley could.

Chapter Three

Sarita had just put the corn bread in the oven when again the sound of a car coming down the drive caught her attention. Setting the timer, she headed to the front door. Through the living room window, she saw the red, convertible sports car come to a halt. A curl of dislike wove through her as the pretty, blond-haired driver emerged. Janice DuPree Corbett was a couple of years younger than Sarita. A member of Katherine's social circle, she considered anyone outside of that circle dirt under her feet and to be ignored.

"Wolf! I had to see for myself. You really are alive," Janice drawled, her expertly made up lips curving into a smile as she approached the porch. "Now, you're a sight I never thought I'd see again."

Choosing not to continue to the front door, but instead moving to the window, Sarita saw Wolf ease himself off the porch railing and into a standing position to welcome the newcomer. Luis rose, also.

Reaching the level of the porch, Janice hugged Wolf.

"I was in Houston all day. When I got home, there was a message on my answering machine from my mother telling me you were back in town. I just couldn't believe it."

Sarita noted that Janice had not even glanced toward Luis.

Realizing his presence was not going to be recognized by Wolf's visitor, Luis reseated himself and returned to his whittling.

Janice's gaze shifted from Wolf to the house. "And why in the world are you staying here?" The implication that this ranch was much too far beneath him was clear in her voice. A sensual smile spread over her face. "You're welcome to come stay with me."

"I don't think your husband would like that," Wolf replied. "Jack and I never did get along."

Janice gave her hair a playful flip. "Jack is ancient history." Her smile became enticing. "I've come to take you to dinner. Mother hired some fancy French chef and let me have Caroline. You always loved Caroline's cooking. She'll make something delicious and we can eat by candlelight on the patio. Then you can decide if you want to stay here or remain with me." She ran her fingers along his jawline. "We should never have quarreled. I only married Jack because I was so angry with you. I never stopped thinking about you."

Capturing her arms before she could wrap them around his neck, Wolf took a step back, putting distance between them. "As tempting as your invitation is, I have to pass on it."

Sarita felt dizzy and realized she'd been holding her breath, waiting for his answer. Gulping in air, she experienced a rush of relief. She'd never trusted Janice.

Again stunned by the protective instinct she was experiencing toward the man, she told herself that he could take care of himself. *On the other hand, any man can be taken in by a pretty face and good figure,* she mused, and her uneasiness returned.

With the uneasiness came frustration aimed at herself. She and Wolf couldn't be in the same room for five minutes without fighting. Why should she care so much about what he did? *What he does is his business, not mine!*

Refusing to give up without having the last word, Janice took a step toward Wolf, raised up on tiptoes and kissed him lightly on the lips. "In case you change your mind, I'm leaving the invitation open." With a final flirtatious smile, she strode back to her car and drove off.

"I apologize for Janice's bad manners," Wolf said to Luis, as they watched the sports car disappearing in the distance.

Luis shrugged. "She's still angry with me for refusing her offer of a job. I explained to her that I'm an old man and can only do so much, and Mrs. Jessip needed me more. Susan Jessip can't work her garden any longer and she needs the vegetables. But Mrs. Corbett didn't want to take no for an answer. She doubled the amount she'd offered. Still, I had to refuse."

Wolf nodded. "Janice likes having things her way."

Luis looked up at him and grinned. "Most women do."

Sarita had continued on to the front door to inform the men that dinner would be ready momentarily. "But most of us are tolerant and understand that you men have to have things your way once in a while," she tossed back at her grandfather.

Wolf raised a skeptical eyebrow. "You? Under-standing and tolerant?"

She frowned, as much at herself as at him. "I am *most* of the time." She didn't add *except where you're concerned,* but the thought did flash through her mind.

"She's telling the truth," Luis said. "She's got a good nature for a woman. Don't know why you two could never get along. Right from the beginning, seems as if you declared war on each other. Sort of like you were born natural antagonists."

"Makes it even more of a puzzle that she'd be stop-ping by my grave."

Luis looked up at Sarita in surprise. "You've been stopping by Wolf's grave?"

Hiding the surge of anger Wolf's telling her grand-father about her early-morning visits caused, she gave a shrug of indifference. "I always go by Mom's, Dad's and *Abuela*'s to say good morning on my way to work. Figured since no one else would remember him, I would." Not wanting to give either of the men a chance to continue this subject, Sarita added, "I've got to get back to the kitchen before my corn bread burns. Dinner will be on the table in five minutes."

Luis frowned as the door swung closed behind her. "My granddaughter is a constant source of amaze-ment."

"I always thought she was just a hardheaded brat who grew up into a difficult woman." Realizing he'd spoken aloud, Wolf grimaced. "No insult intended. That's just the way she used to act when I was around."

"You did bring out the worst in her," Luis con-ceded.

"I still do. We can't seem to be in the same place

for more than a few minutes without getting into an argument." Wolf shook his head. "Doesn't make any sense that she'd go stopping by my grave."

"If you're asking me to explain my granddaughter's actions, you're asking the wrong person. A long time ago I decided that it could drive a man insane to try to understand what makes a woman tick. So I just enjoy them when they're happy and stay out of their way when they're angry."

Following those guidelines, I should made certain Sarita's path and mine never cross, Wolf thought. And that might be the smart thing to do. He could find another place to stay. But he wanted to be near his land. Besides, he liked it here. He felt comfortable with Luis. The old man respected other people's privacy. He never pried and didn't offer unasked-for advice. As for Sarita, Wolf's curiosity remained strong. "We'd best be getting into dinner," he said.

A few minutes later as they sat eating, a question Wolf had avoided asking nagged at him. Of everything he'd left behind, only two things had remained strong in his mind. The first had been his half sister, Claudia. In spite of Katherine's constant attempts to make certain her daughter did not form any bond with Wolf, he'd always felt protective toward his half sister and had wondered how she'd fared. Bradford had informed him that Claudia was attending a private, very exclusive girl's school in Dallas. That she wasn't under Katherine's constant influence had been good news.

But he did not expect good news about the subject of his second concern and had avoided asking. Now he could avoid the question no longer. "I went by the stables earlier today. They look like they haven't been used in years."

"Your father got rid of the horses soon after you were declared dead," Luis replied.

Wolf was hearing what he expected. Neither his father nor Katherine rode. For as long as Wolf could remember, Katherine had tried to get his father to close the stables and get rid of the animals, but Frank O'Malley had felt bound to his deathbed promise to Willow that he would maintain the stables and provide horses for Wolf to ride. That had only increased Katherine's hatred of them. "What happened to Blue Thunder?"

"Since he was getting on in age and he wouldn't let anyone but you ride him…"

Wolf shoved his chair away from the table, his appetite gone. "He had him put down, didn't he?" he growled around the lump in his throat. "Katherine must have been pleased." Before either Sarita or Luis could respond, he rose and strode out of the room.

Since returning to the kitchen, Sarita had begun recalling the man Wolf had been before he'd been in the crash. By twenty-two, he'd grown cold, harsh, cynical and distant. And although, for his sake, she was glad he hadn't been enticed back into Janice's arms, she was beginning to wonder if he was capable of caring about anything or anyone other than finding ways to antagonize Katherine.

Now she knew she was wrong. The man was capable of caring a great deal. The pain she'd seen in his eyes told her that. Racing after him, she caught up with him in the hall. Grabbing hold of his arm, she forced him to stop. "Blue Thunder didn't get put down. *Abuelo* and I took him. He's in the canyon enjoying his old age." Feeling his shudder of relief, she realized she was still holding on to him. Releasing him, she was surprised when her hand continued to remain warm from the contact. Shoving both hands into the pockets of her jeans, she took a step back, putting distance between them. "And seeing that you're back, you can reclaim him. But you don't have to worry about moving him right away. He can stay in the canyon as long as you like."

"You kept him?" he asked, finding this turn of events difficult to believe. "Luis was always complaining about his attitude, and Thunder bit you."

"So he's high-strung. A lot of horses are. My *abuelo* understands that. As for the bite, Thunder and I made peace after that."

Seeing Luis approaching, Wolf's gaze traveled between them. "I'm grateful the two of you didn't let him be put down."

"You've got Sarita to thank more than me," Luis said from behind her. "Not that I like seeing any horse put down. But there's expenses in keeping one. A man in my position has to be practical. But Sarita said she'd pay for any maintenance, and she made it clear my life would be hell if I didn't let her have her way."

Wolf's gaze returned to Sarita. She was proving to be more complicated than a Chinese puzzle. "Why?"

Sarita shrugged. "I don't know for sure," she replied honestly. "I guess maybe I figured I did owe you and him thanks for finding me that day." Not wanting to continue this discussion, she gestured toward the kitchen with a twist of her head. "I suggest we finish our dinner while it's still hot."

Wolf smiled crookedly. "That's as good a thank-you as anyone could deliver. And I will reimburse you for your expenses."

Again experiencing a curious, uneasy curl deep

within, Sarita frowned. "It doesn't mean I forgive you for that endless lecture."

Wolf shook his head. "You're as prickly as barbed wire. Always have been and looks like you always will be."

"Comes from being raised by two men," Luis said, leading the way back to the kitchen. "She didn't have anyone to teach her how to be soft and feminine."

"I can be just as feminine as the next woman when I want to be," Sarita snapped. Catching the skeptical look exchanged between the two men as they seated themselves at the table, she picked up her plate and glass. "I'm eating on the porch."

Without a backward glance, she headed to the front door. Sitting in a rocking chair, her feet propped up on the rail, she glared out at the landscape as she ate. So maybe she didn't know how to flirt as well as some, and she was no good at playing fragile and helpless— that didn't make her any less of a woman.

She heard the screen door open, but refused to look to see who had come out.

"I'm sorry if I made you so angry that you weren't comfortable sitting at your own table," Wolf said, coming to stand where he could see her face. "Taking jabs at each other seems to come natural for us."

She looked at him then. There was honest apology on his face. The frustration she'd been experiencing off and on all day bubbled to the surface. "I don't know why it was so important to me to keep Blue Thunder or why I visited your grave. You'd think, considering our history, I wouldn't have been affected by your passing. Maybe even thought 'good riddance.' Until today we've barely spoken since we were fourteen. So, maybe I did feel bad about not thanking you for finding me that day. As for Blue Thunder, I knew it was your stepmother who wanted him put down and I've never liked her.'' But as she said this, deep down inside she knew that wasn't true. She'd saved Blue Thunder because he had meant so much to Wolf. And another truth refused to remain ignored. She'd gone by Wolf's grave because she'd missed him. It wasn't rational but it was true.

Again Wolf noted that she didn't appear happy about the obligations she'd felt toward him or Blue Thunder. But he owed her for keeping his horse alive, and maybe his crack about her femininity had been a little unfair. ''As I recall, you don't look so bad in a dress.''

Startled by this sudden change in subject, she stared at him in confusion as a slow curl of pleasure began to weave its way through her.

''Just my way of trying to make peace between us,'' he said in answer to the question in her eyes.

The glow of pleasure died. His remark hadn't been a compliment. It had been an appeasement. ''Do you think that's really possible?'' she asked dryly.

''Could be that it's not. Could be that your granddad's right and we're natural-born antagonists. But we could give a truce a try.'' He held his hand out toward her. ''Shake on it?''

She'd never enjoyed being at odds with him. The thought of making peace appealed to her. ''My guess is that this will be an exercise in futility, but I'm always game for a challenge and this should be a big one.''

As his hand encased hers, his touch felt like fire, igniting concern. ''Are you running a temperature?'' she asked, setting her plate aside and rising so that she could press her free hand against his forehead. His temperature was normal. ''I guess not.'' Freed from the handshake and breaking the contact with his face, she frowned in confusion. "Your hand seemed so hot."

"Could have been nerves. Us declaring a truce has got to have been a shock to your system," he quipped.

"True," she agreed, reseating herself and picking up her plate.

And mine, too, Wolf thought. Her touch on his forehead had felt incredibly soothing...an effect he'd never expected to experience from her. "Will you join your grandfather and me?"

"I'll come in for dessert," she replied, wanting a little more time on her own.

Figuring he'd done all he could to promote peace, Wolf nodded and headed to the door. But as he passed her chair, he had the most tremendous urge to give her pigtail a pull. *Talk about residual childish urges,* he mocked himself, recalling how in his youth he'd given in to that urge once and been rewarded with a punch in the stomach. *I came to make peace not war,* he reminded himself and continued inside.

"Sarita still mad at us?" Luis asked when Wolf entered the kitchen and again took his seat at the table.

"She's agreed to a truce between me and her," Wolf replied.

"Considering the way you two have bickered from the time you were tots, keeping that truce seems about as probable as a leopard changing its spots."

So we're all three in agreement on that point. A sour taste filled Wolf's mouth, and he realized that he'd been hoping the truce would last. He was tired of the animosity between him and Sarita. Or maybe he was feeling a little desperate for allies. Mentally, he chastised himself. Katherine had taught him to stand alone. He didn't need anyone but himself.

Finishing his stew, he rose from the table and set his plate in the sink. "I'm going to take a ride out to the canyon and see Thunder."

"Your saddle is in the barn. Your daddy gave it to me along with Thunder. You can take my horse," Luis offered.

"Thanks, but I'll use the Jeep Bradford loaned me." At the door, he paused and looked back. "Thanks again for not letting my father destroy my horse."

"Like I said, you have Sarita to thank more than me," Luis returned.

Life takes some pretty peculiar twists, Wolf mused as he continued out the back door to a rear parking area where the old Jeep Wrangler Bradford had loaned him was parked next to Luis's ancient truck and a well-cared for, older model Ford. He'd never thought he'd be beholden to Sarita Lopez for anything.

Sarita heard the sound of a car engine starting up. It wasn't Luis's truck because it had started without coaxing and it wasn't her car because her grandfather didn't drive her car. It had to be the Jeep she'd seen through the kitchen window.

Had Wolf decided to take Janice up on her offer of an evening's entertainment, after all? she wondered. The thought that their boarder might be moving out quickly should have brought relief. Instead, she frowned worriedly. Janice Corbett was a user and a manipulator. "What Wolf O'Malley chooses to do with his life is none of my business," she again told herself sternly.

But when the Jeep didn't come around the house, and she heard the sound of its engine disappearing in the distance, she breathed a sigh of relief. *Good choice,* she thought, feeling certain he was on his way to the canyon.

"Wolf's on his way to see Thunder." Luis confirmed her assumption, coming out the screen door carrying two pieces of apple pie. Handing her a plate, he added, "He probably had some thinking to do. A horse or a dog can be the best listener when you've got something on your mind."

Sarita gave him a wry look. "That's because they can't talk back and tell you when you're heading in the wrong direction."

"They let you figure that out for yourself."

"And what if you don't want to figure that out for yourself? What if you're hell-bent for trouble?"

"You figure Wolf is hell-bent for trouble?"

"Anyone who tangles with Katherine is looking for trouble."

Luis studied her thoughtfully. "You sound worried about him. Didn't think I'd ever hear that coming from you."

Silently Sarita admitted she hadn't, either. Aloud she said, "I'd be worried about anyone going up against Katherine."

Luis nodded his agreement. "She's a crafty woman."

"And mean-spirited," Sarita added, recalling the day Frank had given Thunder to her and Luis. Katherine had been there, as well, and had thrown a tantrum. "You can't do that! That horse is a menace. It should be put to sleep," she'd insisted. When Frank had told her that he'd given Sarita and Luis the horse and wouldn't go back on his word, she'd gone to their car in a huff and sat there glaring at all of them.

Taking a bite of her pie, Sarita tried to ignore a fresh

uneasiness that was beginning to grow within. She couldn't. "Do you think Wolf remembers how to get to the canyon?" she asked.

"He's been riding this land all his life. Knows it like the palm of his hand," Luis replied.

He was right. Always there had been an agreement between Luis and Willow that they could ride each other's land. Still... "But it has been six years."

Luis glanced toward her. "You sound like a mother hen."

"You're right," she agreed, wishing she hadn't voiced her concern. It was silly of her to be worried about Wolf. Ordering herself to forget him, she took another bite of pie. Her mind refused to obey, and her uneasiness remained.

"Of course, Red Dawn could use a good run. You haven't been out on her for a couple of days," Luis said, breaking the silence between them.

She looked his way. "So you think Wolf might get lost?"

"Nope. But you're sitting there as stiff as a telephone pole. Figured you could use some exercise."

Sarita didn't need any coaxing. "I'll take care of the dishes when I get back," she said, already on her feet.

"I'll take care of the dishes." Apology entered Luis's voice. "I hope you aren't angry with me for letting Wolf stay here."

The words to tell him that she wished he hadn't, formed on the tip of her tongue. But they went no farther. When she opened her mouth to speak, she heard herself saying, "No. We can always use the extra cash. And, like he said, he and I are both adults now. We should be able to tolerate each other." And the

words rang true to her ears. She was glad that they
were providing Wolf with shelter.

"Maybe you two could even learn to be friends,"
Luis said hopefully.

"Now that might be pushing it," she returned, and
continued into the house to put her plate in the kitchen.

As she saddled Red Dawn, the thought that her
grandfather might be considering doing some matchmaking between her and Wolf crossed her mind. "If
that is the case, then he really is getting desperate,"
she muttered.

A short while later she reined Red in. Ahead of them
was the narrow mouth of the canyon. Wolf's Jeep was
parked in front of the wide wooden gate that kept
Thunder inside. "Looks like he didn't have any trouble
finding the place," she said. Then, giving Red a nudge,
she turned her in a new direction and urged her back
into a run.

Darkness was fast approaching by the time she returned to the barn. As she rode in, her attention went
immediately to the vehicles parked behind the house,
and she noted that the Jeep was back. The relief she
experienced was noticeable. *I am not his baby-sitter,*
she told herself.

Leading Red into the barn, she rubbed her down,
then brushed her before going inside. She didn't lie to
herself. She wanted it to be late enough when she went
into the house that she could bathe and go directly to
bed. She and Wolf had never been relaxed in each
other's company, and the thought of sitting around trying to appear relaxed in his presence didn't appeal to
her.

Entering the house, she found Luis in the kitchen.

"Wolf's gone to bed," he told her. "Said he had a busy day tomorrow."

She guessed that Wolf had concluded that the best way for them to maintain their truce was to avoid each other. Glad they were both of the same mind, she headed into the bathroom for a long, hot shower.

Chapter Four

Sarita braced herself for the inevitable as she entered the café the next morning.

"We heard Wolf O'Malley is staying at your place," Gladys said without even her usual "good morning" greeting.

"And Becka Renoldo told her sister that she saw both Katherine O'Malley's and Janice Corbett's cars heading that way," Jules added, coming out of the kitchen almost at a jog.

Becka Renoldo was an elderly woman who lived about a mile and a half down the road from Sarita's home. She sat on her porch a large part of the day watching the world go by, and although she wasn't a gossip, her sister, Thelma Jones, was. Anything Becka told Thelma spread like wildfire. "Yes, he's renting our spare room. And yes, both Katherine and Janice stopped by for a short while, and that's all there is to tell," Sarita said, slipping past Jules and continuing into the kitchen to find her apron and tie it on.

"That can't possibly be everything," Jules insisted, following close behind. "There had to be fireworks when Katherine showed up."

"Very few. She just wanted to make certain Wolf had really returned. She offered to buy him out. He refused and she left."

"And Janice? What did she want, as if I don't already know?" Gladys asked. "She's always looking for trouble, and she and Wolf used to be an item. Was she trying to rekindle the old flame now that Jack is history?"

Recalling the blonde throwing herself at Wolf caused an acid taste in Sarita's mouth. "Yes." Sarita meant to stop there but heard herself adding, "And if you ask me, it would be Wolf who is buying the trouble if he decides to take her up on her offer."

Jules's eyes gleamed with interest. "You're saying he didn't?"

"I'm saying that he didn't take her up on her offer last night. I have no clue what he plans to do today. I'm just saying I think he'd be smart to steer clear of her."

Jules let out a low whistle. "If she's after him, that would take a lot of willpower. She's one great looker and rich, too."

"Men!" Sarita grumbled. "You'd walk right into a rattlesnake den if a pretty woman was leading the way."

Jules breathed a wistful sigh. "Been there, done that."

Gladys laughed. "Sounds as if you don't regret it much."

Jules's manner became sage. "We live. We learn. It's part of life."

"Learning everything the hard way seems like a pretty stupid way to live," Sarita snapped.

"Not 'everything.' But where women are concerned, no man can be certain what to expect. You are all an adventure and one I am glad I have not missed."

Janice Corbett wasn't an adventure, she was a fast ride to destruction, Sarita thought, but she had no desire to continue this discussion. "Customers should be arriving soon," she said. "I'm going to check on the tables."

Following her out of the kitchen, Gladys drew her aside where Jules couldn't see or hear them. "You aren't attracted to Wolf O'Malley, are you?" she asked with concern.

Sarita gave her an "are you crazy" look. "Of course not."

Gladys frowned uneasily. "It's just that you sounded so adamant about his not getting mixed up with Janice Corbett."

"I wouldn't wish her on my worst enemy." Sarita abruptly grinned cynically. "Well, maybe if I really wanted them to suffer."

Gladys continued to look concerned. "Wolf O'Malley has a cold streak that scares me. Not that I blame him. Losing his mother at such a young age and then having Katherine as a stepmother. That could turn anyone bitter."

Sarita put her arm around Gladys's shoulders. "Don't worry. I am a sane, rational person who does not go looking for trouble."

Gladys breathed a sigh of relief. "Good. Now that I've done my sisterly deed for the day, we can get the tables ready."

* * *

Wolf parked in the semicircular drive in front of the house his father had built for Katherine. It had been designed to resemble the antebellum plantation houses in *Gone with the Wind*. He'd never felt welcome inside its walls.

"Because I wasn't," he mused, recalling that Katherine had insisted the construction be started immediately following the wedding. She'd said they needed a fresh start and then gone about trying to erase Willow O'Malley from Frank's memory. Other than those Wolf insisted on keeping in his room, every picture and personal possession of Willow's had been boxed up and put in the attic. There had not been much. All of her clothes had been given away during the months following her death. Along with the photos there had been a few pieces of jewelry and the silver brush, comb and mirror set Frank had given her on their first anniversary.

Wolf had overheard Katherine trying to convince Frank that he should sell the jewelry and toiletry set, but he'd insisted that Wolf might want it some day. Katherine had not been happy. She was jealously possessive of Frank and wanted no evidence that he'd ever loved anyone else. It was because Wolf had been a constant reminder that he had, that she'd hated him so much.

Wolf had realized this and knew his father must have also. But Frank was flattered by Katherine's jealousy. Besides, any attempts he made to change her were futile. Because he loved her, he played referee between her and Wolf, trying always to minimize the tension by keeping them apart as much as possible. But his actions had made Wolf feel more and more like an intruder in his father's home.

Glancing at his watch, Wolf noted that it was just half past eight. With anyone else he would have called before showing up at such an early hour, but he preferred not to give Katherine time to prepare.

Climbing out of the Jeep, he strode to the front door and knocked.

Ralph Avery answered. In his sixties now, lean, with a thick head of white hair, he was the epitome of the English butler. His wife, Loretta, was the housekeeper, and the two of them had kept the O'Malley household running smoothly for nearly thirty years.

"Master Wolf. Congratulations on your survival," he said, his manner remaining staid, his voice its usual polite monotone, giving no evidence of emotion.

Flashes of memory whisked through Wolf's mind. It had been with that same expression and tone of voice that, through the years, Ralph had annually wished him a happy birthday and congratulated him when he'd graduated from high school and from college. At times like that Wolf had wondered if the man ever experienced any depth of feelings. And Loretta was much the same way. They reminded him of bookends…silent, sturdy, doing their jobs without question or emotion.

"Thank you, Ralph," he replied.

Ralph acknowledged Wolf's words with a slight, almost indiscernible nod. "If you will wait in the drawing room, I'll inform Mrs. O'Malley of your arrival."

"Thanks." Heading into the drawing room, it occurred to Wolf that "thanks" and "thank you" were pretty much the extent of his vocabulary with Ralph. He had tried in his youth to have a conversation with the man, but Ralph always simply replied, "yes, sir" or "no, sir" or "I don't know, sir" to whatever Wolf had said, then gone on his way.

In the drawing room Wolf stood frowning at the furnishings. They were too frilly, too feminine for his taste. A wry smile curled one corner of his mouth. In his youth he'd been banned from this room. Katherine had claimed he always smelled of horses, and she didn't want that odor getting into her furniture. Thinking back, his room had been the only room in the house in which he'd felt comfortable. When his father had sent him away to military school, he'd actually experienced a sense of relief.

"And to what do I owe this visit?" Katherine asked, striding into the room. "Have you decided to sell me your land and your share of the business and be on your way?"

"I've come for mine and my mother's things."

Exaggerated mock regret showed on her face. "I'm afraid they're gone. I needed storage space."

Wolf's gaze hardened. He'd expected this, still it angered him. "And where have they gone to?"

"The dump. By now they are an integral part of our landfill."

He read the pleasure in her eyes that this was giving her. "Some day you will regret your vindictiveness."

She smiled. "And you will regret having threatened me." Reaching for the sleeve of her dress, she yanked hard, ripping it. "And assaulting me in my own home," she added, reaching up and combing her fingers into her hair.

Realizing the mistake he'd made coming here alone, Wolf glared at her. "You haven't changed one bit."

She pulled her fingers out of her hair, freeing strands from the chignon at the nape of her neck so that she looked mussed as if she'd been in a struggle. "Do you prefer to wait for the police here, or shall I send them out to the Lopez place?'' She began to work her voice into a sob as she reached for the phone.

"Madam." Ralph's impersonal tones interrupted.

Both Wolf's and Katherine's gazes jerked to the door.

"How long have you been there?" Katherine demanded.

"Since you entered. I thought you might be going to request refreshments," he replied, continuing to regard the scene with blank emotion.

Wondering how strong the man's loyalty to Katherine was, Wolf asked, "Did you happen to notice how Mrs. O'Malley's dress got ripped?"

"Yes, sir."

"If questioned by the police, would you lie for her and say I did it?"

"I would say that I assumed she had a bug on her sleeve and accidentally ripped it trying to kill the insect. She has never been fond of bugs."

"How very observant of you," Katherine said. Then, tossing Wolf a hostile glance, she whisked out of the room.

Wolf continued to regard Ralph coolly. "I would never have credited you with being so quick-witted. You saved your job, Katherine's dignity and kept me out of jail."

Ralph took a step into the room and lowered his voice. "In this household, a person must be prepared to guard their back at all times, sir." Stepping back through the doorway and into the hall, he motioned toward the exit. "If I were you, sir," he said, letting his gesture speak for itself.

Outside, Wolf breathed in a breath of fresh air and vowed never to confront Katherine alone again.

Back behind the wheel of the Jeep, his hand went to the string of beads with the totem of the bear that hung around his neck. It, the picture of his mother he carried in his wallet and her land was all he had left of Willow Bluefeather O'Malley and her family.

His jaw hardened. Katherine could erase all the physical evidence of his mother's existence that was within her grasp, but she could never erase that which was in his heart.

By mid-morning Sarita was getting very tired of fielding questions about Wolf. "If there's ever anything I want everyone to know, I'll be certain to tell Thelma Jones," she grumbled under her breath to Gladys.

"Look on the bright side. We've never been so busy. I'll bet I make double my usual amount of tips today," Gladys whispered back.

She was right about that, Sarita acknowledged. This should have been the lull before the lunch crowd. At most on a normal day there would be two customers. Today the place was half-full. "Every coffee klatch in town must have decided to come here instead of hanging around their own kitchens today. It also looks like all the regulars from Angelica's Tea Shoppe decided they preferred Jules's coffee today."

Gladys grinned. "Everyone wants to be where the action is."

"Well, the only action they're going to get around here is having their food served to them."

"Maybe not."

Sarita glanced over her shoulder in the direction of Gladys's gaze and saw Wolf and Bradford Dillion entering. Bradford's usual table was unoccupied, and they headed for it.

"Darn!" Gladys fumed. "I was hoping for a close-up look at Mr. O'Malley."

"Be my guest."

Gladys's smile returned. "You can have table three. Old Mrs. Palmer is getting on my nerves. I hate the way she taps on the floor with her cane when she wants service, reminds me of being back in the library in high school. Remember the way she'd give that cane a hard rap on the floor if she heard anyone whisper even one little word? She's one of Angelica's customers I hope doesn't come back here."

Sarita remembered the librarian well. Everyone did. Anyone who crossed her went straight to the principal's office and was given a day's detention. All of the students were certain he was afraid of her as well and didn't dare not punish anyone who irritated her. She'd even had the history teacher barred from the library for a semester because the woman was constantly taking reference books to her classroom and not returning them the same day. When she'd retired five years ago, it was rumored that the faculty, administration and students alike had breathed a collective sigh.

Three rings by Jules on the counter bell told Sarita that the food for table three was ready. She was serving it when a sudden hush came over the café. Looking toward the door, she saw that Preston O'Malley had entered. Three years younger than Wolf and a stark contrast in appearance, he was blond, blue-eyed, with a boyishly handsome face and the ability to charm the fuzz off a peach. Today, however, his usual friendly demeanor was replaced by a scowl that deepened as he strode through the room. Coming to the table where Wolf was seated, he stood glowering.

"Morning, Preston," Wolf drawled, when the younger man remained silent.

"Don't you ever go near my mother again," Preston seethed, his tone implying that Katherine needed protection from Wolf.

Wolf's jaw hardened into a cold line as he rose from his chair. "You'd better get your facts straight before you go implying something that's a lie. This time I don't intend to sit back and let Katherine get away with her games. I'll take you to court and sue you for slander. Or did she forget to mention that Ralph was a witness to our conversation?"

For a moment Preston's self-important air wavered, then a sneer of disgust spread over his countenance. "You are not welcome in our home. Stay away."

"I went to your mother's house to collect mine and my mother's things only to discover they had been entirely disposed of."

"We assumed you were dead. That left no one who would have wanted pictures or any mementos of a filthy Indian squaw and her half-breed son. Besides, they were stinking up the attic."

Sarita saw the cold control on Wolf's face replaced by rage. His hand balled into a fist, and she knew he was going to take a swing at Preston, proving to everyone that he was as dangerous as Katherine and her son wanted people to believe. A part of her wanted to interfere, while another part, as angry as Wolf about Preston's description of Wolf and Willow, wanted Wolf to knock Preston flat.

Suddenly a loud, sharp rap of a cane caused her to jump, and she saw her own startlement reflected on the faces of the other patrons as all eyes turned to table three and Mrs. Palmer.

"Preston O'Malley, I should have thought you would have better manners," the elderly librarian said, rising to her feet, her voice carrying the same commanding authority Sarita remembered. "Someone should wash your mouth out with soap." Her gaze shifted to Wolf. "I recall your mother vividly. She was a fine woman, pretty, polite and kind to everyone." Her gaze shifted back to Preston. "You would have benefited greatly from having known her."

"Witch!" Preston breathed under his breath and, turning on his heels, strode out of the café.

Wolf's gaze continued to rest on the librarian. "Thank you," he said. "For my mother and for keeping me from doing something I would have regretted."

"I merely told the truth," she replied. "And if I didn't need this cane to balance, I'd have taken a swat at his behind for you." Then, reseating herself, she began to eat.

As Wolf, too, returned to his seat, Sarita drew a relieved breath and headed into the kitchen to make up a salad for table four.

"Sounded to me like Preston came in spoiling for a fight," Jules said as she entered his domain. "Kind of stupid if you ask me. Wolf's got at least four inches and twenty pounds on him."

Gladys had joined them, and in a lowered voice said, "Maybe he wanted to be injured. He'd do anything to please his mother."

Both Jules and Sarita raised questioning eyebrows.

"I heard Bradford Dillion warning Wolf that if Wolf had hit Preston, Preston could've pressed assault charges," she elaborated. "Then Wolf said that maybe that's what Preston had wanted and maybe Katherine had put him up to it."

Jules frowned. "I find it hard to believe any mother would put her son in that kind of danger. Even if it was only one punch, Wolf could have done some real damage."

"Preston probably came up with that on his own," Gladys agreed.

Recalling the hatred she'd seen in Katherine's eyes, Sarita wasn't so sure. "If Wolf is smart he'll stay away from both of them."

As both Jules and Gladys nodded their agreement, she picked up her freshly made salad and left.

The general chatter among the customers had resumed. Glancing toward Bradford's table she saw that Wolf was missing. A couple of minutes later when Gladys approached the men's table to refill their coffee, Bradford covered Wolf's cup.

"He left," Gladys whispered disappointedly into Sarita's ear as she whisked past on her way to another table.

Sarita expected to feel relieved. Instead, she found herself worrying that he was on his own with no one to protect him from Katherine and Preston. *He can take care of himself,* she told herself sternly. Still, her uneasiness lingered.

By the time she was on her way home, her nerves were taut. Passing Becka's place, she saw the white-haired woman sitting on her porch, rocking. Usually Sarita waved. Today anger that Becka was acting as a watcher for Thelma kept her from making the friendly gesture.

Nearing her home, she saw Wolf sitting on the front porch, and relief washed through her.

"Been waiting for you," he said, rising as she neared.

The grim expression on his face caused her to tense once again.

"Bradford mentioned that you always waited on his table. I've been wondering why you sent Gladys over. If I'm making you so uneasy you don't want to even wait on me in a public place, maybe I should find another place to bunk," he continued in a cool drawl.

Considering the disconcerting effect he was having on her, the thought that it might be best if he did leave occurred to her. But she didn't want him going for the reason that he thought he made her uneasy. "Gladys asked me to switch tables with her. She said Mrs. Palmer made her nervous." This wasn't a lie, just a slight readjustment of her conversation with Gladys.

Wolf's expression relaxed. "Just didn't want to be hanging around if you wanted me gone."

"Your being here or not being here makes no difference to me." *Liar!* her inner voice chided, as again she was forced to realize that she didn't really want him to leave. *All right, so his presence adds a little excitement to life,* she reasoned, admitting that her existence had fallen into a dull routine before his resurrection from the grave.

"Good." He lowered himself back into the chair. He'd been prepared to leave, if that was what Sarita had wanted. Now he realized that he'd wanted to stay. He liked it here. Funny, he thought, Sarita Lopez's home was the last place he would have thought he'd feel comfortable.

She meant to go on inside, instead she heard herself asking, "Do you really think Preston was trying to provoke you into hitting him?"

Wolf recalled the blond-haired waitress lingering around their table a little longer than was necessary. "Gladys doesn't miss much, does she?"

Feeling as if she was the one who'd been caught eavesdropping, Sarita flushed. "No. Sorry I asked."

As she started to walk away, he frowned at himself. He hadn't meant to make her feel uncomfortable. "Let me ask you something."

Surprised that he wanted to continue their conversation, Sarita paused at the door and turned back. "What?"

"Preston was only sixteen when I left. He was spoiled and thought he was better than everyone else. But he was his mother's son, he knew how far he could push people, and he never placed himself in any danger. Has he changed so much that he would go inviting a punch in the face?"

Sarita thought for a moment, then said, "I've never seen him do that before." Recalling her youthful encounters with Wolf, she was forced to add, "But then I don't know how the two of you got along before you left. Word was that you didn't."

"No, we didn't. But he generally steered clear of me." He frowned at the landscape in the distance. "Today I saw that same malicious gleam in his eyes that I've seen in Katherine's. In answer to your question, yes, I do think he was deliberately trying to provoke me into hitting him."

"Then I'm glad you didn't."

His gaze swung to her and he smiled. "Me, too."

His smile was disconcerting. *Because he so rarely smiles in my presence,* she reasoned. Recalling something else Gladys had said, she asked, "Do you honestly think Katherine put him up to it?"

"It's possible. She tried to pull a stunt on me that would have gotten me arrested if Ralph hadn't been there. And she was furious that her plan was thwarted."

"When Katherine dislikes someone she can be vindicative," Sarita conceded. "But I still find it hard to believe she'd send Preston to be injured. She dotes on him."

"It's possible he thought it up himself, to please her," Wolf said.

"I'd buy that before I'd believe she sent him to be hurt." Sarita told herself that she'd pried enough, but her curiosity was too strong. "So what kind of stunt did Katherine pull?"

"She ripped the sleeve of her dress and mussed her hair. It was obvious she was planning to tell the police I'd assaulted her. But before she could reach the phone, Ralph suddenly said something from the doorway, letting her know he was there."

"And he'd seen everything?"

"Everything."

Sarita pictured the staid butler. "So what did he say?"

"He said that if asked he'd tell the police he assumed Katherine had spotted a bug on her shoulder and accidentally ripped her dress trying to kill it."

"Kept his job but got you out of hot water."

Wolf nodded.

Sarita couldn't stop herself from asking, "Did his expression change? I've never seen anything but one polite, bland look on his face."

Again Wolf grinned. "Nope. His expression never changed. But he did speak more than a couple of words at one time."

Sarita grinned back. "I've often wondered about his and Loretta's courtship. Of course she is so much like him, I suppose they took one look at each other and realized they were kindred souls."

"I doubt you could find two individuals who matched each other better," Wolf agreed. His grin broadened. "How about that. We've been talking for more than five minutes and aren't at each other's throats."

"A true miracle," she quipped back, realizing that she was actually feeling comfortable in his presence. Suddenly recalling the angry exchange between Preston and Wolf, sympathy entered her voice. "I am sorry Katherine destroyed yours and your mother's things."

Wolf's grin vanished. "She's a spoiled, possessive woman. She hated the idea that my father could have loved another woman. Any evidence that my mother and I even existed has always been distasteful to her."

"Well, if I were you, I'd make certain I was never alone with her," Sarita cautioned.

"That's at the top of my list." Anger at all Katherine had robbed him of again surfaced, and his gaze shifted back to the arid landscape. "But I won't let her run me off again. This land is as much a part of me as it was of my mother."

"It does get a hold on you. I've never wanted to live anywhere else."

"You've always been too set in your ways," Luis grumbled coming out of the house at that moment. "That's why you don't have a husband."

Sarita didn't want to get into that discussion with him in front of Wolf. "I'll go see what we've got to fix for dinner," she said, continuing into the house.

"Didn't hear any shouting," Luis noted as he eased himself into his chair and picked up his whittling.

"Wasn't any," Wolf replied, then fell silent. He felt calmer than he had all day. That talking to Sarita had accomplished that amazed him.

In the kitchen Sarita stood staring with unseeing eyes into the refrigerator. The thought that Wolf O'Malley had a very nice smile was occupying her entire mind. Abruptly she shook her shoulders. *Don't get used to it,* she warned herself. This truce between them wouldn't last. The only reason they hadn't fought today was because they had Katherine to talk about. If their conversation ever began to revolve around themselves, sparks were bound to fly.

The sound of a vehicle approaching caught her attention. What now? she wondered. Guessing the caller was someone looking for Wolf, for a moment longer she continued to survey the interior of the refrigerator. Then her curiosity got the best of her. Shoving the refrigerator door closed, she headed to the front of the house.

Through the living room window, she recognized Jeremiah Jordon's old beat-up truck. Jeremiah, a hulk of a man in his late forties, who made his living doing odd jobs and hauling trash, climbed out. He wasn't the brightest person in town, but he was one of the most honest and reliable.

"Afternoon," Luis called out to the man.

"Afternoon. I've come to see Mr. Wolf." Jeremiah approached the porch slowly, watching Wolf as if not certain it was safe to get too close.

"It's good to see you again, Jeremiah," Wolf said, rising and leaving the porch to offer the man his hand in greeting.

Now knowing he was welcome, Jeremiah's hesitant expression turned to one of pleasure. "It's good to see you too, Mr. Wolf. Sure was sad to hear you'd died." He frowned as if mulling this around in his mind. "But then you didn't really."

"No, not really," Wolf conceded.

Sarita stepped out on the porch. "Can I get you something cold to drink?" she offered.

"Oh, no, ma'am," Jeremiah called back. "I just came to see Mr. Wolf." He suddenly grinned. "Mrs. Katherine don't think I'm too bright and she's right, but I ain't stupid, neither." His gaze rested on Wolf. "I was doing some repair work on the garage roof today when she calls me in. She says she'll give me a hundred dollars to take some boxes to the landfill. And she makes me promise I'll take them there. So I says sure. Then she leads me up to the attic and tells me which ones to take."

"This happened today?" Wolf asked, hoping he was right about what he was guessing was in the boxes.

"Yes, sir. Just before I ate my lunch." His tone became conspiratorial. "She told me I couldn't look inside. But Mr. Ralph, he came up to the attic after she left, and he looked inside. Then he tells me that what's inside belongs to you. That they're your heritage, and he shows me what's inside. They was full of pictures of you and your mama and other stuff...personal treasures is what my mama calls them. And Mr. Ralph says you should have them." Jeremiah frowned. "But Mrs. Katherine, she'd told me that I had to take them to the landfill, and I'd promised her I would."

Knowing how easily Jeremiah could be frightened, Wolf fought to keep his voice level. "The boxes are at the landfill?"

Jeremiah's grin returned. "They was there, but they're not there no more. I'm a man of my word. Everyone in this town knows that. I took them out to the landfill, like I promised I would." His grin broadened. "But she never made me promise I'd toss them in. They's in the back of my truck. Just been on a little ride."

Wolf clasped the man's hand. "Thank you, Jeremiah. I owe you."

"No, sir. Miss Katherine paid me enough."

"Then you give this to your mother for teaching you about respecting people's personal treasures." Taking out his wallet, Wolf extracted a hundred-dollar bill and gave it to the man.

"She'll like this, sir. She always says what goes around comes around and being nice to people brings niceness back."

"Don't ever forget that," Wolf said. "Now, let's unload those boxes."

As they started lifting the boxes out of the truck, Sarita realized her eyes were filled with tears. Under the circumstances, being happy for Wolf was a normal reaction. But being so happy she was in danger of crying shocked her. They weren't that close friends. They weren't even really friends.

Afraid the tears might spill out and that he'd see them and think she was silly for overreacting, she went back inside and busied herself preparing dinner.

Chapter Five

Wolf woke the next morning with the feeling of being truly at home. He'd stayed up late the night before, going through the boxes Jeremiah had brought. The framed photos of his mother, her father and himself that had once adorned his bedroom, he'd placed on the bureau and the nightstands. The string of beads that had been a birth present to him from his maternal grandmother, he'd hung on the corner of the mirror. And there was a wooden bowl his grandfather had helped him carve. In the past he'd used it to hold whatever came out of his pockets...change, his pocket knife, wallet, et cetera. And now it sat on the bureau performing that same function. Everything else was still in the boxes, except for a single loose photograph he'd retrieved from a shoe box of photos that had been among his mother's things.

Shifting into a sitting position, he picked it up from the nightstand beside his bed where he'd laid it just before going to sleep and frowned at the two children standing in front of a corral. They were him and Sarita at what he guessed was around six years of age. The pose was friendly. He had his arm around her shoulders, and they both were smiling. As hard as he tried, he could not recall a single time in their lives when they'd been on such good terms.

Rising, he dressed and went into the kitchen. Luis was sitting at the table, his breakfast dishes pushed to one side while he drank coffee and read the morning paper. Sarita was seated there, also, eating a bowl of oatmeal. Both glanced his way as he entered. The greeting on Luis's face was open and friendly. Sarita's expression was polite but guarded, as if she expected trouble between them at any moment. And, he admitted, he was on his guard where she was concerned.

"I found this among my mother's things," he said, casually dropping the photo on the table between them as he continued past and poured himself a cup of coffee.

Unable to control her curiosity, Sarita picked it up first. Disbelief spread across her face. "This has to be a fake."

Luis reached out for it and she handed it to him. Looking at it, he chuckled. "I'd forgotten about this."

Wolf stood, leaning against the counter. "Well? So what happened?" he coaxed, when Luis said no more.

The old man chuckled again. "As usual, you two were ignoring each other. That was your way of abiding each other's presence. Your mama decided to play peacemaker. She dared the two of you to be civil to each other for the entire afternoon." Luis shook his head. "Of course that didn't work. You two were too smart for that. So she tried bribing you. You were each going to get a silver dollar. And you were doing real well until Willow decided to take that picture. Guess getting that close was just too much. As soon as the picture was snapped, you gave Sarita's pigtail a pull. And she punched you in the stomach."

"Must be an ingrained urge," Wolf muttered. "Just last night I was tempted to do the same thing."

Sarita frowned at him. "I can't believe a grown man would even consider doing that."

"It was just a momentary lapse. I remembered the punch in the stomach. You have quite a wallop."

Luis laughed. "Yep. She sure does. I told Willow she should have gotten a picture of that. It'd be more normal. But she just shook her head and said she guessed hoping you two would be friends was futile."

Wolf's attention turned to the dark-haired woman at the table. "I'd like to think she was wrong." As his words echoed in his mind, he knew they were true.

Sarita studied the rugged features of the man in front of her. "Me, too," she conceded.

"Well, that sure sounds like a good start to me," Luis declared.

Wolf nodded his agreement, and Sarita experienced a surge of joy. Again shaken by the intensity of her reactions to this man who had been an antagonist for so many years, she felt a need to escape. "I've got to get going or I'll be late," she said, rising from the table.

Wolf was certain he'd seen honesty in her eyes when she'd said she too wanted to be friends. But as she prepared to leave, he read a guardedness in her. He couldn't fault her. "I feel like we're embarking on a long and arduous journey that may or may not take us where we want to go," he said, letting her know he too had his doubts.

Her pleasure lessened. "I suppose that's as good an analogy as any."

A short while later Sarita paused at her father's grave on her way to work. "You would not believe the events of the past couple of days. Wolf O'Malley and I are living under the same roof." Her expression turned grim. "You used to say that he and I were natural-born enemies. But I find myself wanting to be his friend. Maybe it's because he needs friends right now, and I've always been a champion of the underdog." Her face screwed into a crooked frown. "I know it's probably hard, no make that impossible, to think of Wolf as being an underdog. But you have to remember that he's fighting Katherine."

In her mind's eye, she saw her father nodding sagely. He'd been an expert carpenter and had done work for the O'Malleys on several occasions. And he'd always been glad when the job was done. "Katherine O'Malley is one woman who scares me," he would say after a day at the estate. "There's a coldness in her eyes that lets you know she considers you less than an insect and will willingly crush you under her foot if you don't do exactly as she asks." Then he would always add, "But the money's good."

Continuing on her way, she recalled that her father had also often remarked about how smitten Frank O'Malley was with his wife. "But then Katherine is an entirely different person with him," he'd say. "She's all sugar and spice. Has him completely bamboozled. But then love can do that to a man. He sees what he wants to see."

"Too bad for Wolf that his father didn't see the truth about Katherine," Sarita murmured under her breath.

But then, maybe he had and had simply ignored it. Frank O'Malley had not been stupid or naive. But he had been in love, and, as her father had said, love could cause a man not to want to admit the obvious.

A red sports car passed her at that moment. It looked like Janice Corbett's car headed out of town in the direction of her grandfather's place.

A sudden concern for Wolf filled her. *He's a big boy. He can take care of himself,* she again told herself. Besides, that couldn't have been Janice. It was too early for the woman to be up and out. Janice was, no doubt, still in bed or at the most just beginning to sip on her first cup of coffee. Still, the thought of men being foolishly blind where a pretty face and good figure were concern taunted her.

Wolf had just finished washing his breakfast dishes when the sound of a car coming down the drive caught his attention.

"Looks like company for you," Luis said, entering the kitchen and continuing out through the back door.

It's clearly someone he doesn't want to say "good morning" to, Wolf mused as he headed to the front porch.

Seeing Janice Corbett climbing out of her car and approaching, he had to admit she was a good looking woman. And sexy. This morning she was wearing a pair of blue jeans that looked as if they'd been molded on her and a tank top that showed off the fullness of her breasts.

"Thought you might like to go for an early-morning ride," the blonde said as she reached the porch. "There's a couple of gorgeous Thoroughbreds out at my daddy's place that could use some exercise."

Wolf's gaze raked over her. He knew she'd worn the jeans and tank top just for him. Normally when she went riding she wore a riding habit from the pages of the trendiest fashion magazines. And he had to admit that he was flattered. But he wasn't naive. Janice usually had a self-serving reason behind everything she did. Or it could be that she was simply bored and considered him a fresh diversion. Either way he had some time to kill. "A ride sounds like fun."

Triumph gleamed in her eyes. She motioned toward her car with a twist of her head. "Great. Climb in."

"I'll follow you. I have an appointment with Bradford later this morning." He didn't, but he wanted his own transportation and a reason to avoid spending the entire day with her.

A few minutes later as he drove behind her, he grinned wryly at himself. There had been a time when he would willingly have devoted an entire day to trying to bed her. Now she was offering him an open invitation and he found himself uninterested. He thought back to yesterday and how she'd ignored Luis. She'd always thought she was better than others. In their youth he'd accepted her spoiled behavior. Now he found it distasteful. A truth suddenly struck him. She was very much like Katherine.

He lost interest in being a diversion for her. However, there was still the possibility she had a more serious motive in mind and, if so, he was interested in finding out what that was.

When they parked near the stables he saw two horses, saddled and waiting. "You were very sure of yourself," he said, joining her as she climbed out of her car.

"I never allow a man to reject me twice in a row,"

she purred, running her fingers seductively along the line of his jaw.

He was not certain what tipped him off, but he was suddenly convinced she was not merely looking for a way to fill her day with a little excitement. She was up to something. "Shall we..." He motioned toward the horses with a wave of his hand.

"Are you sure you wouldn't prefer to ride something a little softer," she cooed.

"And take the chance of your father catching us? I don't think so. He never liked me."

"He and mother are in Europe."

She was trying way too hard to seduce him. Slipping an arm around her waist, he guided her toward the horses. "I'd really like to go for a gallop. It's been a long time."

Her mouth formed a pretty pout. "You're still mad because I married Jack, aren't you?"

Deciding to use that excuse for his standoffishness, he said, "Let's just say you taught me to be a bit more cautious where women are concerned."

She smiled, clearly flattered that she'd made such a strong impression on him. "Then I suppose it's up to me to teach you to trust again."

I'd trust Sarita Lopez before I'd ever trust you. Startled that Sarita had entered his mind, he realized that she was the kind of woman a man could trust. There was no subterfuge about her. But now was not the time to be thinking about Sarita. He needed to keep his full attention on Janice. Returning her smile, he said, "That won't be easy."

Sliding her arms around his neck, she went up on tiptoes, her mouth heading toward his. "I'm always game for a challenge."

Capturing her arms and freeing himself before she could kiss him, he said firmly. "Shall we get mounted?"

"That was what I had in mind," she returned with a seductive pout.

"The horses," he clarified.

"So you are determined to play hard to get." She laughed confidently. "Well, that will just make winning more fun."

Not wanting her to guess that he'd rather go to bed with a rattlesnake, he smiled back noncommittally.

"So what were you doing all those years in the wilds of Alaska?" she asked as they walked to the horses and mounted.

"Learning the basics of survival." The statement came out too curtly. He saw the flash of uneasiness in her eyes. *Don't scare her off before you find out what she's up to.* "And what have you been doing while I've been gone?" he asked in friendly tones.

Invitation again returned to her voice. "Getting rid of Jack, then waiting for someone to come along who could hold my interest."

Wolf again found himself thinking of Sarita...caring for her grandfather, working, cleaning house, doing laundry, having very little idle time. He felt a curl of irritation that she had to work so hard to survive while Janice had all her needs met with a mere flick of her hand. "Sounds boring."

"Well, I did do charity work, and there are parties one is expected to throw." She sighed as if this was more work than one person should be required to handle.

Again Wolf found himself comparing her pampered life-style to that of Sarita's. Sarita won the points. He frowned. Why Sarita Lopez kept popping into his mind puzzled him. Shoving her out, he concentrated on Janice. She ran in the same crowd as his stepmother. It could be that she knew something about Katherine that he could use if his stepmother chose to wage war against him. "Do you see much of Katherine?"

"We occasionally run into each other at parties and charity teas."

Janice's tone of voice implied that she and Katherine were barely on speaking terms, but Wolf recognized the tiny little twitch at the corner of her mouth before she answered. She was lying. Was she doing a bit of spying on him for Katherine?

"Are you planning to stay in town?" Janice asked.

"Yes. And I plan to take an active interest in all phases of the family business." If she was Katherine's spy, this was as good a way as any to let his stepmother know the full extent of his intentions.

For a minute or two they rode in silence, then Janice said, "Your father was grooming Preston to take over his place."

Wolf fought back a surge of irritation. "My father started teaching me the business when I was twelve. From the time I was sixteen, I was on the payroll. I know the business from top to bottom."

"You must realize that Katherine wants Preston to take your father's place. She'll vote her shares with him, and she has control of Claudia's shares until Claudia turns twenty-one."

"The way I remember things, Preston doesn't like working. He prefers to party. Henry Jarrot owns forty percent, and he's too greedy to let the business go under. Katherine might intimidate him, but his love of money is more powerful than any fear of her."

"You're probably right," Janice conceded. She smiled wryly. "Katherine's not going to like this."

Wolf regarded her thoughtfully. He had no doubt now that she'd been spying for Katherine. But the amusement in her eyes told him that for her this was merely a game, and he was fairly certain she didn't really care who won. She was in it for the entertainment. "So tell me, what you think of my stepbrother as a businessman?"

"Preston, as he puts it, doesn't like the nitty-gritty of business. He considers himself an idea man."

That sounded like Preston, Wolf mused. He knew his stepbrother well. He'd had to. Preston had spent his youth trying to get Wolf into trouble. He was clever and manipulative and had always considered himself better than others. Preston must have been looking forward to being in a position of power. Recalling his encounter with his stepbrother the previous day, Wolf wondered if Preston's rage had really been because his own plans were now in danger. Well, he'd known he would have to battle both Katherine and Preston when he returned. "I suppose investing in a spa is one of Preston's ideas. I doubt my father would ever have considered it, and it's definitely not Jarrot's style."

"The spa isn't going to be part of O'Malley Jarrot Enterprises. It's a separate investment, set up by Katherine, Preston and Greg Pike."

Wolf was stunned that his stepmother would be striking out on her own in the business world. "My father wasn't involved?"

"Katherine never mentioned it until after his death."

"Until after she thought she owned my mother's property." Katherine's final revenge. His mother had loved her land as it was...wild and untamed. And although, in his heart, he knew she would not mind if he built a home on it, she would have hated the thought of it being turned into a plush resort for the wealthy.

"Well, it was just sitting there unused."

Talk of Katherine was grating on his nerves. Wolf nodded toward the horizon. "Race you to the dry riverbed."

Acceptance of the challenge in his voice glistened in Janice's eyes. In the next instant she'd kicked her horse into a gallop.

The hard riding relaxed Wolf, clearing his mind. Revenge wasn't Katherine's entire motive, he conceded, recalling overhearing Luis telling Sarita that Pike was still interested in their property for the spa.

Suddenly worried that Pike might sweeten his offer to one Luis was tempted to accept, he said, "I've got some business I need to take care of," and turned them back toward the stables. He did not want Katherine anywhere near his property.

Janice eyed him with interest. "That certainly came up suddenly. Was it something I said?"

"No. Just something I should have thought of earlier," he replied, and again nudged his horse into a gallop.

Returning to Luis's place, he saw Pike's car parked in front and Pike on the front porch talking to Luis. "Got back not a minute too soon," he murmured under his breath.

"I've increased our offer as far as is practical. It's triple what any Realtor will tell you the land is worth," Pike was saying as Wolf approached. "If you're waiting for more, it's not going to come. Our price is more than fair."

"Whatever he's offering, I'll offer more," Wolf said, reaching them.

Pike glared at him. "What in the hell do you want this property for? Can't believe you're interested in building a spa."

"Thunder likes the canyon the way it is. I just want to make sure he has a good home until he passes away."

Pike gave a disgusted huff. "He isn't even your horse anymore."

"Sure he is," Luis corrected. "Sarita and I have just been looking after him."

Pike turned to the old man. "We'll best any offer you get."

"I'm not selling." Luis's gaze shifted between the two men. "Course if Sarita was to get married, I'd most likely be giving her a big chunk, including the canyon, as a dowry."

Knowing how humiliated Sarita would be if she ever learned that her grandfather had attempted such a tactic, a startlingly strong protectiveness toward her coursed through Wolf. "You don't need to buy a husband for Sarita. I'm sure she can find one on her own."

"She hasn't done such a good job so far," Luis returned.

Wolf pictured Sarita. She was a strong, proud woman and what her grandfather was doing could hurt her deeply. His anger toward Luis increased. "She's not going to take kindly to this."

Luis shrugged. "In my day every girl had a dowry. For some it was just a few cooking utensils or some linens. For others it was more. I'm simply following the tradition of my ancestors."

"I don't think Sarita will see it that way," Wolf

growled, amazed that his desire to defend and protect her was growing even stronger.

"Then I would suggest we don't tell her." Luis's gaze again shifted between the two men. "If either one of you breathes a word of this, I'll sell the land to the one who kept our little secret."

Greg smiled reassuringly. "You don't have to worry about me. Keeping secrets is part of a lawyer's job." His grin broadened. "I've always thought your grand-daughter was a fine-looking woman. A little strong willed and sharp-tongued, but worth the effort, I'm sure. I best be on my way. I've got some courting to do."

As the lawyer's car pulled away, Wolf glowered at Luis. "You can't be serious, but, if you are, Sarita has a right to know what's going on."

"If you're so concerned about her, maybe you should consider doing a little courting yourself."

Him and Sarita? They'd need to give each other sparring gloves for wedding presents. Wolf shook his head. "This is going to backfire."

"She loves this land, but that's not the real reason she stayed here. Before her father died, she was going to go away to college or maybe nursing school. After he died, nothing I said would make her go, even for a short while. On his deathbed he'd made her promise she would take care of me. She was at an impression-able age and took him much too literally. Now I have a chance to take care of her."

"Buying her a husband isn't the way to do that."

Luis gave him a wry look. "I'm an old man. I'm desperate. Like I said, if you're so worried about Greg Pike as a husband for her, you could court her. You

tamed Thunder. You can tame Sarita. And you will
have the canyon as a reward.''

"I would never consider marrying a woman for a
piece of land. And I didn't tame Thunder. We came to
an understanding. Besides, as you've already noted,
Sarita and I are natural-born antagonists." These last
words tasted unusually bitter on his tongue.

"So, I could be wrong. Maybe the two of you could
change if you're willing to work at it. Maybe you could
bury the hatchet and come to an understanding. It's up
to you. As for me, I've done my duty by my granddaughter."

Wolf shook his head at the old man once again and
went inside. Pike, he knew, could be charming when
he wanted to. And he'd heard Sarita confessing that
she would like a husband. The frown on his face deepened. He hated the thought of her getting hurt and that
was what was going to happen if she fell for Pike's
line. The man was a womanizer, always had been. And,
he wasn't the type to let a wedding ring stop him. "I
owe her for keeping Thunder alive," Wolf murmured
under his breath, searching for a reason that would explain the depth of his concern for her welfare. Silently,
he vowed that he would keep an eye on the situation.
If she looked as though she was heading for trouble,
he'd find some way to stop her.

Chapter Six

"**G**ood afternoon."

Sarita looked up from the table she was wiping off to see Greg Pike standing beside her. "If you've come to ask me to talk to my grandfather about selling his land, the answer is still no." Letting him know she considered this conversation over, she returned to wiping the table.

"I didn't come to talk to you about your grandfather's land. I came to have a quiet cup of coffee."

Sarita straightened and turned back to him. He was smiling warmly, and there was a gleam of interest in his eyes.

"You're looking very nice today," he added, seating himself without ever taking his eyes off her.

Sarita's suspicions prickled. He'd never considered her worth even a first look before. And she wasn't his usual type. He preferred his women sophisticated, beautiful and wealthy with an emphasis on the *wealthy*. "One cup of coffee coming up," she said coolly.

"Greg here to pester you again about your father's land?" Gladys asked in a whisper, joining Sarita by the coffee machine.

"He says not."

"Then why are you looking as if you're considering pouring that coffee in his lap?"

"I could swear he's trying to flirt with me."

Gladys grinned dryly. "I never thought we lowly commoners were his type."

"Me, neither." Sarita's voice became chipped ice. "If he's planning to come calling on me to win favor with my grandfather, he'd better come up with another ploy."

"Some men will do anything to get what they want," Gladys said under her breath.

Sarita gave her a wry glance. "Gee, thanks."

"I didn't mean that as an insult. I just meant that some men will use others without considering who they hurt."

"Well, Greg Pike isn't going to play any games with me," Sarita vowed.

"Maybe I should serve him that coffee," Gladys suggested, a hint of fear that Sarita might actually pour it on the man in her voice.

"I'll take care of waiting on him." Sarita turned back to the table where Greg was sitting to find him watching her, open masculine interest on his face.

"If it will take that hostile gleam out of your eyes, I'll tell you that we've decided to forget about your grandfather's land. We're looking at another plot on the other side of town," he said as she placed the coffee in front of him.

She continued to eye him suspiciously. "If you're saying that, hoping we'll suddenly panic because you've withdrawn your offer and agree to sell, you're mistaken. My grandfather is not playing a game. He doesn't want to sell his land...period.''

"I know. And we've accepted his decision.''

Sarita had to admit he looked as if he meant it. Still... "You do and you have?''

"Yes, and yes.'' He smiled warmly again. "So can we be friends?'' He held out his hand to her.

"I'm not sure about us ever being friends. We don't run in the same circles.''

"You're a difficult woman, Sarita Lopez.'' He continued to hold out his hand. "Friendly acquaintances, then?''

He seemed determined, and she didn't want to be rude. "Friendly acquaintances,'' she conceded, accepting his hand. The contact was firm and strong, and he held on a fraction longer than was necessary. It was definitely a flirtatious handshake.

Retreating to the kitchen, she studied him covertly through the serving window.

"What's going on now?'' Gladys asked.

"Something going's on?'' Jules demanded, his tone indicating his displeasure at being the last to know.

"I don't know.'' Sarita frowned at the handsome brown-haired man drinking his coffee and jotting down notes on some papers he'd taken out of his briefcase.

"Sarita thinks Greg Pike might be trying to court her to get in good with her grandfather so Luis will sell him his land,'' Gladys explained.

"The cad!'' Jules snorted.

"Apparently, I was wrong about that,'' Sarita confessed. "Just now he told me they've decided to forget about my grandfather's land and that they're looking at a site on the other side of town.''

Gladys eyed her speculatively. "So maybe his having to deal with you caused him to take a second look, and he liked what he saw."

"Ah, romance," Jules chimed in.

Sarita gave him a look. "The man's a skirt chaser, always has been. He's never been able to stay monogamous longer than six months that anyone has known of." She turned to Gladys for confirmation.

"He does have a problem with commitment," Gladys conceded. "His marriage lasted less than a year." The speculative glimmer remained in her eyes. "But then you're not his usual type. Maybe you could domesticate him."

"Trying to change a man is like trying to change a leopard's spots," Sarita returned.

"I thought you women enjoyed that kind of challenge," Jules noted.

Sarita shook her head. "Not me. I've never been one to hit my head against a brick wall until I drew blood." Without giving either a chance to respond, she left the kitchen. Picking up the coffeepot on her way past the counter, she continued on to Greg's table and refilled his cup.

"Once you get to know me, I'm a nice guy," he said. "How about dinner? My way of apologizing for harassing you about the land."

Sarita stared at him in disbelief. "You actually want to take *me* out on a date?"

His gaze traveled over her and his smile warmed with appreciation. "You're a good-looking woman. Why wouldn't I want to date you?"

He made her feel desirable. Still, she wasn't ready to trust him. "I'm not your usual type."

"So maybe I'm bored with my usual type." Challenge flickered in his eyes. "Maybe my taste is changing. You do look delicious."

"I'm not dessert," she returned coolly.

"No. You're definitely a full-course meal."

Sarita had heard the door opening. Now she was experiencing a prickling on the side of her neck. Glancing to her right, she saw Wolf approaching.

Arriving at Greg's table, his gaze flickered from one to the other, while his expression remained shuttered. "Afternoon."

"Sarita and I were having a private discussion," Greg said with dismissal.

Ice crystallized in Wolf's eyes as his gaze leveled on Greg. "Don't know what the two of you would have in common. She's an honest woman. You don't know the meaning of the word."

"I'm considering letting her teach me. You know...the good-hearted woman turns the charming cad into perfect husband material."

Wolf's gaze swung to Sarita. "You're too smart to buy that, aren't you?"

Her rational side was, but his assumption that Greg Pike couldn't possibly be truly interested in her raised her ire. "You probably think that any man who would ask me out is either insane or has ulterior motives."

"I didn't say that." Mentally Wolf kicked himself for interfering so quickly, but the thought of her even being touched by Greg Pike turned his blood cold. "You're too good for the likes of him."

Sarita couldn't believe what she was hearing. Wolf O'Malley was paying her a compliment. Even more startling was the way her heart was suddenly pounding double time with excitement. Looking hard at Wolf, she found herself thinking that he was incredibly hand-some.

"And I suppose you think you would be better for her?" Greg asked caustically. "I'd like to point out that I didn't disappear for six years and let everyone think I was dead."

"I have no intention of making a play for Sarita." Wolf placed an arm around her shoulders. "But you can consider me her overly protective big brother who'll beat you to a pulp if you hurt her."

For a moment the firm musculature of his arm was all Sarita could think about. Then something that felt very much like disappointment swept through her. This was followed by anger. She wasn't certain who she was most angry with—herself for thinking Wolf might be interested in her as a woman or him for butting unin-vited into her life. Stepping free of him, she gave him a haughty glare. "I have no need for a big brother. From what I've heard, some can be a real pain in the neck, and it's my guess you'd fall into that category."

The mention of necks caused Wolf's gaze to go to hers and he found himself wondering what the area just below the hollow behind her ear would taste like. In the next instant he was picturing the slap in the face she'd deliver if he did try for a sample. "I'm just trying to keep this guy from taking advantage of you."

They'd come full circle again, she mused. Using concern for her welfare as an excuse, he was trying to boss her around again. "No one is going to take ad-vantage of me."

"You see, O'Malley, she's a woman with a mind of her own." Greg grinned at Sarita. "I admire that. So how about letting me prove that I want to change my ways...find a woman who's sincere and honest."

Sarita frowned. "From what I've heard, you're the one who is usually lacking in sincerity and honesty in your relationships with women."

He continued to grin at her. "Come on, take a chance. One date can't hurt anything. I'll feed you well. I know a great place in Phoenix. The food is fabulous, and they have a band that plays on Friday and Saturday nights. We can dine and dance the night away."

Wolf found the thought of the lawyer's arms around Sarita repulsive. "I'm sure Sarita has better things to do with her time than waste it on you."

"Everyone should waste a little time once in a while on frivolous activity," Greg countered.

It occurred to Sarita that it had been a long time since she'd done anything frivolous. And, admittedly, she was still irked by Wolf's sudden urge to play big brother. "You're right," she said to Greg. "What time do you want to pick me up on Saturday?"

He smiled triumphantly. "Six okay?"

"Six," she agreed, then turning sharply, headed back to the kitchen.

Bootsteps followed in her wake.

"I can't believe you agreed to go out with that man," Wolf growled as the kitchen door swung closed behind him.

"Jules Desmond." Jules introduced himself, stepping between Wolf and Sarita. "This is my place and I don't allow brawls."

"This isn't a brawl," Wolf stated curtly. "I just want to know what insanity suddenly came over Sarita."

She glared at him over Jules's shoulder. "You've always thought you knew what was best for me. You act like I don't have an ounce of good sense. There is nothing insane about wanting to have a good time."

Ignoring the human barrier between them, Wolf glowered at her. "Greg Pike is not to be trusted."

"I have no intention of falling for the man. But a nice dinner and dancing sounds like fun. *And*, I don't need a big brother to look after me. I can look after myself just fine."

"That remains to be seen," Wolf growled, turning so sharply he almost collided with Gladys who had just entered. Making a brisk apology, he strode out of the kitchen and out of the café.

Jules sank into a nearby chair. "My knees have never felt so weak."

"What happened in here?" Gladys demanded.

"I put myself between Wolf O'Malley and Sarita to protect her. I never realized how big he is. He could have snapped me in two," Jules wailed.

"He wouldn't have hurt you," Sarita assured him.

"Convince my knees of that. They still don't want to support me," he returned. "I can understand why people think he pushed his stepmother down those stairs."

Sarita glared at him. "He did no such thing."

"So why was he angry with Sarita?" Gladys demanded, bringing the conversation back to her original question.

"He was playing big brother. Greg Pike asked me out on a date, and Wolf doesn't want me to go. He thinks I can't take care of myself," Sarita elaborated.

Gladys and Jules stared at her in disbelief. "Greg Pike asked you out?" they said in unison.

She experienced the sting of insult. "I don't understand why everyone is so shocked. I'm not that ugly, and my manners are passable."

"We know that," Jules said quickly. "It's just that you aren't Greg Pike's type."

"So he's decided that he wants to try a new type," she retorted.

"But do you really want to get involved with him?" Jules's voice held a note of caution.

"No. At least, I don't think so. But then maybe I need a change. My life has fallen into a rut."

Gladys placed an arm around Sarita's shoulders. "Just be careful. I don't trust him."

"Neither do I," Sarita confessed.

"Then why go out with him?" Jules demanded.

Because Wolf O'Malley doesn't want me to, was the answer that popped into her mind. But that was too childish to admit. An alternative she preferred came to mind, which was equally the truth. "I suddenly found myself wanting to do something different. Besides, what harm can one date do?"

"None, I suppose," Gladys replied. Abruptly she grinned. "You can tell us how the other half lives."

"Don't let him talk you into anything you don't want to do. I've seen men like him operate. They're real smooth manipulators," Jules cautioned.

"I promise I won't do anything rash," she assured him.

Walking home that afternoon, she began to have her doubts about going out with Greg. By the time she reached the house, she was ready to call and cancel their date.

Luis looked up from his whittling as she mounted

the steps. "You look like someone with a heavy load on your mind."

Certain he would disapprove of her even considering going out with Greg, she shrugged. "It's nothing important. I was going to do something, and now I'm not. It's over and done with."

He frowned. "I hope you're not planning to call off your date with Greg Pike."

Suspicion etched itself into her face. "How did you know about that?"

"I told him," Wolf said, coming out the door.

The angry look he shot at Luis told her that he was not pleased with her grandfather's reaction. She, herself, was stunned. Her gaze swung to Luis. In the past he'd never had a good word to say about Greg. "You actually want me to go?"

Luis smiled. "If there's any good in the man, I'm sure you're the one who can bring it out."

Sarita was having a hard time believing her ears. She'd expected Luis to object strongly, instead he was encouraging her. "And what if there isn't any good in him?"

"Then you will have wasted one evening. You have no husband or children. You've got the time to spare."

Wolf issued a loud "humph" and continued off the porch. "I'm going to the canyon to see Thunder. The way I see it, right now he and I are the only rational beings on this ranch."

Luis chuckled at his departing back. "Seems a mite upset by your date."

Sarita frowned. "He's just mad because I wouldn't let him bully me into doing what he wants me to do."

Luis's expression became serious. "I do think he's truly concerned about your welfare."

"I know. He told Greg he was taking on the role of my big brother." Again the sharp jab of disappointment that announcement had caused pierced her. More angry with herself than with Wolf, she added, "The last thing I need is a big brother, especially Wolf O'Malley."

"Heard he went riding with Janice Corbett this morning."

"Then I'd say he needs a big sister to look after him a lot more than I need a big brother to look after me," Sarita returned, and went into the house. Once alone, she started to reach for the phone and call off her date with Greg, but before her hand closed around the receiver, she stopped. Pride refused to allow her to let Wolf think he'd bullied her into seeing things his way.

Ordering herself to put both men out of her mind, she busied herself with laundry and preparing dinner. But Wolf's and Greg's images continued to plague her.

She was forced to admit that she was flattered by Greg's unexpected attention, but she was also wary. In romance novels a man who'd known a woman all his life would suddenly see her in a new light and realize he loved her and even the worst cad changed his ways to win the woman of his dreams. But this wasn't a novel, and she couldn't honestly visualize Greg changing his ways. Most likely he'd become bored with the women in his own circle and was seeking a new adventure. Well, he was going to discover that she'd meant it when she said she didn't play games.

As for Wolf, she had no need for a big brother, and she would make that clear at every opportunity. But it wasn't his role as big brother that really nagged at her. It was the thought of him and Janice together. The woman was poison; her former husband would attest to that. "I'd worry about any man she set her sights on," Sarita declared, justifying the concern she was experiencing for Wolf.

Going out onto the back porch to ring the dinner bell, she wondered if Wolf had returned from the canyon. If not, she'd put a plate in the oven for him. "With any luck that will be the case," she muttered under her breath. "Then *Abuelo* and I can have a quiet dinner without his irritating presence."

But a few minutes later as she and her grandfather sat down alone, she found herself missing Wolf's presence. *How can I possibly be missing that man?* she fumed silently. In her mind's eye she saw him standing beside Thunder—strong, sturdy and ruggedly handsome. Bullheaded, arrogant and a know-it-all, she added curtly, shoving the image from her mind.

But when she heard his Jeep approaching, a flow of joy that he was back washed through her. *I'm just relieved that I don't have to do two sets of dishes,* she told herself sternly.

"Sorry I'm late," Wolf apologized, passing through the kitchen on his way to the bathroom to wash up.

Sarita began to fork her food into her mouth double time. The roller-coaster ride he was giving her emotions had her wanting to escape his company as quickly as possible.

"You're going to choke if you don't slow down," Luis cautioned. "A person might get the impression you're afraid of sharing a table with Wolf."

She stopped. "I am *not* afraid." Slowing to a snail's pace, she awaited Wolf's return.

"Heard you went riding at the Corbett place," Luis said, when Wolf had eased himself into his chair and begun dishing food onto his plate.

WELCOME TO THE
CASINO!

Try your luck at the Roulette Wheel ...
Play a hand of Twenty-One!

How to play:

1. Play the Roulette and Twenty-One scratch-off games, as instructed on the opposite page, to see that you are eligible for FREE BOOKS and a FREE GIFT!

2. Send back the card and you'll receive TWO brand-new Silhouette Romance® novels. These books have a cover price of $3.50 each in the U.S. and $3.99 each in Canada, but they are yours to keep absolutely free.

3. There's no catch. You're under no obligation to buy anything. We charge nothing — ZERO — for your first shipment. And you don't have to make any minimum number of purchases — not even one!

4. The fact is, thousands of readers enjoy receiving books by mail from the Silhouette Reader Service™ before they're available in stores. They like the convenience of home delivery, and they love our discount prices!

5. We hope that after receiving your free books you'll want to remain a subscriber. But the choice is yours — to continue or cancel, any time at all!

So why not take us up on our invitation, with no risk of any kind. You'll be glad you did!

Play Twenty-One For This Exquisite Free Gift!

THIS SURPRISE
MYSTERY GIFT
WILL BE YOURS
FREE WHEN YOU PLAY
TWENTY-ONE

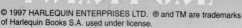

It's fun, and we're giving away *FREE GIFTS* to all players!

PLAY ROULETTE!

Scratch the silver to see that the ball has landed on 7 RED, making you eligible for TWO FREE romance novels!

PLAY TWENTY-ONE!

Scratch the silver to reveal a winning hand! Congratulations, you have Twenty-One. Return this card promptly and you'll receive a fabulous free mystery gift, along with your free books!

YES!

Please send me all the free Silhouette Romance® books and the gift for which I qualify! I understand that I am under no obligation to purchase any books, as explained on the back of this card.

Name: _____
(PLEASE PRINT)

Address: _____ Apt.#: _____

City: _____ State: _____ Zip: _____

The Silhouette Reader Service™ — Here's how it works:

Accepting your 2 free books and mystery gift places you under no obligation to buy anything. You may keep the books and gift and return the shipping statement marked "cancel." If you do not cancel, about a month later we'll send you 6 additional novels and bill you just $2.90 each in the U.S., or $3.25 each in Canada, plus 25¢ delivery per book and applicable taxes if any.* That's the complete price and — compared to the cover price of $3.50 in the U.S. and $3.99 in Canada — it's quite a bargain! You may cancel at any time, but if you choose to continue, every month we'll send you 6 more books, which you may either purchase at the discount price or return to us and cancel your subscription.

*Terms and prices subject to change without notice. Sales tax applicable in N.Y. Canadian residents will be charged applicable provincial taxes and GST.

If offer card is missing write to: Silhouette Reader Service, 3010 Walden Ave., P.O. Box 1867, Buffalo, NY 14240-9952

BUSINESS REPLY MAIL
FIRST-CLASS MAIL   PERMIT NO 717   BUFFALO NY

POSTAGE WILL BE PAID BY ADDRESSEE

SILHOUETTE READER SERVICE
3010 WALDEN AVE
PO BOX 1867
BUFFALO NY 14240-9952

NO POSTAGE
NECESSARY
IF MAILED
IN THE
UNITED STATES

"Figured I could use a good ride. Thunder's too old to carry me."

Luis nodded his understanding. "If you're in the market for a horse, you might want to contact Hank Jefferies. He's got a two-year-old stallion...not as much spirit as Thunder but solidly built."

"I'll look into it. I contacted George Evans today. He's going to come out and get the stables back into shape." Wolf's gaze turned to Sarita. "I want Thunder to sire a foal. I spent a little time with your mare this afternoon. She's about as feisty as any I've seen. I think she'd be a good match. I'll pay good money."

A curl of sensual excitement wove through her at the thought of the two horses mating. *There is something definitely wrong with my hormones,* she grumbled to herself. "Sure, why not?" she agreed, keeping her attention on her food.

"Good. I brought him back with me and put him in the corral. I thought we could let them spend some time together. If they don't mate naturally, I'll contact the vet."

Sarita merely nodded and kept eating.

"You thinking of taking up with Mrs. Corbett again?" Luis asked as Wolf began to eat.

Wolf raised an eyebrow indicating he thought that question was a bit too personal.

Sarita flushed. "Really, *Abuelo.* That's not your business."

Luis shrugged off her reprimand. "He's been away a long time. He should know he might be stepping into something he'd rather not get on his boot before it's too late."

"Bradford Dillion has already filled me in on the real details behind her marriage. He told me that during the divorce it came out that after her daddy put her on a strict allowance, she got Jack to marry her by saying she was pregnant, then a couple of weeks after the wedding, she claimed to have a miscarriage. And he made it clear that he thought the whole pregnancy was a ruse."

Sarita looked at him then. "I'd say that your knowing that and still seeing Janice is lot stupider than me dating Greg Pike."

He leveled his gaze on her. "I've known what Janice was capable of for a long time. I've got no delusions about her sincerity, and I know that she's always looked out for herself first."

"Well, I've got no delusions about Greg Pike," Sarita assured him. "So that makes us even in the 'I know what I'm doing' category."

Wolf told himself to drop the subject, but again the thought of her getting involved with Greg Pike rankled him too much to let him remain silent. "The problem is that women let their emotions get the best of them, and Greg can be a real charmer when he wants to be."

"I can't believe that you think I'm so weak-minded that I'd let any man wrap me around his little finger," she retorted.

Wolf studied the woman across from him—the fire in her eyes, the hard line of her jaw. The urge to be the man to tame her swept through him. In the next instant he was chiding himself for such folly. "I do find it impossible to picture you softening for any man," he conceded.

Luis shook his head. "That is what makes finding her a husband so difficult. A man likes a tender, giving woman to tend to him."

"If I marry I'll be tender and giving when that's

warranted," Sarita returned, "but it won't be a one-sided relationship with me giving all and him taking all."

Luis shook his head with disapproval.

Wolf felt sorry for her. Her grandfather was being unfair. "She's right. Marriage should be a fifty-fifty proposition." Again he leveled his gaze on her. "And you won't get that with Greg Pike. He's a user."

That Wolf had come to her defense had pleased her, but that he thought she was so blind as to not see Greg Pike as he was infuriated her. "All I'm doing is going on a date. I'm not walking down the aisle with him," she snapped, and pushing her chair away from the table, she rose and stalked out of the kitchen.

Chapter Seven

Sarita was waiting on Bradford Dillion the next morning when Greg entered. He strode to her and handed her a rose.

"I made Ruth Marley get out of bed and open early just so I could greet the prettiest woman in town with a flower to match her beauty," he said in a voice loud enough to carry to several nearby tables.

Sarita could only stare. He was publicly declaring his interest in her. She'd been certain that at least among his social circle, he would want to keep their date as much a secret as possible. As several of the customers suddenly leaned closer to each other and began to whisper, she flushed. "That really wasn't necessary," she said, finding her voice.

"I thought it was." Taking her hand, he kissed it and left.

"I'd never buy a used car from that man," Bradford said, voicing the opinion Sarita had always held of Greg.

She looked down at the flower. "This is a little much," she conceded. "I wonder what his game is."

"Glad you see that it is a game." Wolf's voice came from behind her. Walking around her, he took a seat at Bradford's table.

She'd left the house early to avoid him this morning. Now the faint scent of his aftershave taunted her senses. "I told you, I'm not stupid."

Stalking into the kitchen, she found a glass and put the rose in some water.

"Mr. Pike does seem determined," Jules noted. "Maybe he's finally taken his blinders off and realizes you're the real thing."

"Or maybe he knows Sarita isn't a pushover like the rest of the bimboettes he dates and he's trying to weaken her," Gladys offered.

Sarita's gaze first turned on Jules. "I doubt he's seen the light." She swung it to Gladys. "And I'm not impressed by a flower." She looked at both of them. "It's just a date. Nothing more."

Both held up their hands like traffic cops stopping traffic. "No more will be said," Jules vowed, and Gladys nodded her agreement.

"Good," Sarita snapped, and headed back out to take care of her customers.

Her hope that that would end any discussion about Greg Pike was dashed almost immediately.

"Greg is an excellent catch," Vivian Kale said as Sarita poured her a fresh cup of coffee. "I have to admit that I'm a little amazed that he'd settle on you but then you are much more of the domestic type than his usual dates. I suppose he's decided it's time to settle down with a woman he can count on to make him a real home and raise his children."

"It's just a date," Sarita declared between clenched teeth. "That's all. I'm just going on a date with him."

Vivian eyed her dubiously. "But I would have thought he'd find someone with a little milder disposition." A sudden light shone in her eyes. "Unless he's using you to make someone jealous. He was seeing Tammy Brown until she took up with Vance Goodman."

Sarita glared down at her, and in a voice loud enough to carry to anyone else in the café who was listening, she said, "Don't you have anything better to do with your time than speculate about other people's lives?" Turning, she addressed the rest of the assembly. "Yes, I'm going on a date with Greg Pike. But it's just a date. It doesn't mean anything, and I don't want to hear anyone else's opinion. Thank you very much."

Charlie clapped loudly. "You tell them, girl. We all have a right to make our own mistakes. Don't need no busybodies interfering."

Sarita let out a low growl of frustration and retreated to the kitchen to count to ten before she approached his table to refill his coffee cup.

When she returned to her customers, no one said anything more, but still she didn't relax. Her grandfather's reaction to her date with Greg nagged at the back of her mind. He was the only one who hadn't been surprised or negative about it. Something wasn't right.

"Well, look who's back in town," Jules said with pleasure. It was nearly closing time when the petite blond teenager entered and took a seat at the window table.

Sarita looked past him to see Claudia O'Malley. At

fifteen, she was a younger version of her mother, physically. But that was where the similarity ended. Claudia was shy and withdrawn. Because she went to school elsewhere, and because when she was at home her mother allowed her access only to children her own age who were within the upper social circle, she had no close friends in town. Those children she was allowed to socialize with had formed a tight clique, and unless prodded by their mothers so that Katherine would be pacified, they had no time for Claudia.

"Lonely little rich girl" was what Jules had labeled her the first time she'd come into the café and he was right. That described her perfectly. He'd adopted her as his special customer, and when she came in, he would go out and personally find out what she wanted. If she wasn't certain, he would concoct something special just for her. Both Gladys and Sarita had been surprised by his fatherly attitude toward the girl until they'd discovered that Jules had had a daughter who had died in her early teens.

"Tonight I will bake my famous chocolate cake," he announced. "It is her favorite. For today, I shall see what she wants to eat. Perhaps a little linguine."

"It's nearly closing time," Gladys complained. "And you're talking about concocting one of your gourmet creations?"

"We'll lock the doors, and she can eat while you straighten up for tomorrow," he returned, already on his way out of the kitchen to his favorite customer.

Sarita was pouring a final round of coffee for her customers when Jules waved her over.

"Miss Claudia wants only a word with you," he said, studying the young girl with concern. A knowing smile came over his face. "I will bring her an ice cream soda. She must have sustenance."

Claudia smiled up at him. "Thank you, but I'm really not hungry. I just need to speak to Miss Lopez."

As Jules left, shaking his head because she would not even have a soda, Claudia looked up at Sarita. "I've been told that Wolf is staying at your place."

"He's renting our spare room," Sarita replied.

"I was wondering if you would mind if I accompanied you home today. I would very much like to see him."

Sarita recalled that Claudia was the only one of the O'Malley clan to weep openly at Wolf's funeral. "I'm walking and it's a bit of a hike but you're welcome to come with me."

Gratitude showed on the girl's face. "Do you think Wolf will be there when we arrive?"

"I can't be certain, but you're welcome to wait."

Claudia studied her narrowly. "I thought you and Wolf fought all the time. I remember my father saying that if I ever went riding with Wolf and you were at the stables helping your grandfather, I should stand clear."

"Your half brother and I have a truce for the moment," Sarita replied. "A dubious one, but a truce."

"He can be difficult, but he's got a good heart," Claudia declared. "Whenever I was in trouble or needed help, he was there. Of course he had to do it behind Mother's back. She never wanted us to be friends."

Sarita experienced an inner rage at Katherine for working so hard to keep Wolf an outsider in his own family. She'd lost her mother and grandmother at an early age but her grandfather and father had loved her dearly. And when her father had died, she'd still had her grandfather. As for Wolf, he'd had no one after his father had married Katherine. His stepmother had seen to that. For the first time, she truly understood how alone he must have felt.

"I made you an ice cream soda, anyway," Jules said, joining them and setting the luscious drink in front of Claudia. "It's on the house."

She smiled gratefully and brought a flush of pleasure to his cheeks.

Wolf was sitting on the front porch with Luis when Sarita and Claudia came down the drive. A smile of recognition spread over his face as they drew near, and he rose and went toward them.

"This can't be my kid sister," he said when he reached them, looking Claudia up and down.

"Your real one, in the flesh," Sarita returned, reminding him that *she* wasn't.

Casting her a wry smile, he returned his attention to Claudia. "You've grown into a lovely young lady."

She grimaced. "I know I look like my mother, but I'm not like her."

Wolf grinned. "Glad to hear that."

Claudia grinned back, then tears began to run down her cheeks. "I hated it when I thought you were dead. I felt so alone."

"You had your father, your mother and Preston," he consoled, bending down to give her a hug.

She shook her head into his neck. "You know how jealous mother was of Daddy. When he and I started doing things together, she sent me away to school so I wouldn't take up so much of his time. As for Preston, he and Mother are like one, and I might as well not exist. They don't even notice when I'm around.''

"That could be for the best,'' Wolf said, releasing her and straightening. "Preston used to play some very unpleasant practical jokes.''

Claudia nodded. "He still has a real mean streak.'' A plea entered her voice. "Can I come live with you? Mother said you're planning to stay. That means you'll be getting a place of your own, doesn't it?''

"I'm planning to have a home built on my land,'' Wolf confirmed. "And, if Katherine allows it, you're welcome to live with me but I wouldn't hold my breath if I were you.''

Claudia's face brightened. "When I turn eighteen, I can do what I want, and that's less than three years.''

"I don't know if I'd want to be trying to date and have Wolf looking over my boyfriends,'' Sarita muttered.

Claudia grimaced. "It can't be any worse than Mother. Sometimes we're allowed to socialize with the boys from a nearby school. Mother has the head mistress at my school send her reports on the boys I even talk to, then she has their backgrounds checked, and if they don't come up to her social standards, she writes and tells Miss Canterberry that I cannot speak to them anymore. And then Miss Canterberry threatens to expel me if I don't comply.'' A wistful expression played across her features. "Once I considered disobeying, but I knew she would expel me and I'd be sent somewhere else where I didn't know anyone.''

"Poor little rich girl'' did describe her perfectly, Sarita thought.

"Won't Katherine be upset when she finds out you're here?'' Wolf asked.

Claudia shrugged. "I don't think so. I told her that I wanted to see you, and she said I could do as I pleased. She didn't seem concerned one way or the other."

"That doesn't sound like your mother," Wolf noted.

Pride spread over Claudia's features. "Maybe she's realizing that she can't control every move I make."

Wolf doubted that was the case, but said nothing. He would let his half sister have her moment of triumph. "Come on and say 'hi' to Thunder and tell me what you've been doing these past six years." Slipping an arm around her shoulders, he began guiding her toward the stables.

But as they passed the porch, Claudia paused. "Good afternoon, Mr. Lopez. I didn't mean to ignore you when I arrived. I was just so excited to see my brother," she said with polite deference. "I'm glad to see you're looking so well."

"Afternoon, *señorita*," Luis replied with a smile. "And you're looking very well yourself."

She nodded and grinned, then continued around the house with Wolf.

"Nice child. Good manners," Luis said as Sarita mounted the porch.

"Yes, she is." Sarita had wondered if Claudia would notice Luis. The fact that the child had was another mark in her favor.

Sarita sat, her feet propped up on the porch railing. Night had fallen, and the sky was glittering with stars. Wolf had taken his sister to dinner in town. They'd all been somewhat amazed when Claudia had called to tell Katherine of her plans and her mother had raised no objections.

The sound of an approaching vehicle caused her to glance toward the road. Wolf's Jeep was heading toward the house. It was only then that she realized she'd been waiting for him. Mentally she shook her head at how large a part of her life he seemed to have become. *Once he gets his own place built, that will change. He won't be coming around here again.* This thought was supposed to be a comfort. Instead, it depressed her. *Was my life so boring without him that I'm actually going to miss him?* she wondered, watching the Jeep pass in front of her on its way to the back of the house.

Forcing him out of her mind, she stared up at the moon. Maybe going out with Greg Pike wasn't such a bad idea after all. Could be she needed to make a few changes in her life.

"Claudia doesn't seem to have inherited any of Katherine's arrogance," Wolf said, coming out the front door of the house and taking a seat on the porch railing.

Startled that he'd joined her, she found herself stiffening slightly, and her heart raced a little faster. "No, she doesn't."

"I need to ask you something and I want an honest answer."

His tone had turned grim. In the illumination of the porch light, the lines of his face were more deeply shadowed, and she could see that he didn't like what he was about to say. "I'd like to think that the one thing we have between us is honesty," she said.

He nodded his agreement. Guilt prickled through him. He wanted to tell her about the canyon, but his hands were tied. Putting that problem to the side for the moment, he concentrated on his immediate concern. "I've been away a long time. I've missed watching

Claudia grow up. Was her behavior today typical or were you surprised that she was so friendly toward me and showed no arrogance toward you or your grandfather.''

Sarita easily guessed the suspicion that was nagging at him. "You think she might be spying for her mother?''

"You, Luis and Bradford are the only people in this town I feel I can trust." It had amazed him when he'd realized that he trusted her. He'd asked himself why, and realized that in all of their bickering, he'd never sensed any subterfuge.

That he trusted her brought a surge of intense pleasure to Sarita. "Claudia behaved like her usual self. I never realized the two of you had been close, but she did weep openly at your funeral. And I know that what she said about her and her mother is true. At least that's the way it's always looked from the outside."

Wolf nodded. "Thanks." She looked so cute sitting there, he had an unexpected urge to kiss her. *And get myself soundly slapped,* he thought, mocking his desire. Plus he'd probably end up sleeping in the stables. Straightening from the railing, he stood beside her chair. "For whatever reason brought you there, thanks for visiting my grave. It's nice to know someone cared." Unable to entirely fight the desire to test the taste of her skin, he leaned forward and kissed her lightly on the forehead.

"You're welcome," she managed as he disappeared into the house. The heat of his lips was like a brand. When she pressed her fingers against it, heat radiated up her arm, causing her heart to pound faster. "It was just a friendly little peck," she grumbled at herself. But it had left more of an impression than any kiss she'd ever had before.

Clearly her life had been much too much of a routine, stuck-in-a-rut existence.

Later that night, lying in his bed, Wolf heard Sarita moving around the house. Unexpectedly he found himself imagining her coming to his door, knocking and entering. She was wearing a short cotton nightgown and her hair was loose and flowing. Approaching his bed, she climbed in beside him. Startled by the arousal this daydream was causing, he laughed at himself. Bedding her would be like trying to mate with an angry bear. Still, the image stayed with him as he drifted off to sleep.

Late in the night he awoke in answer to nature's call. Groggily climbing out of bed, he pulled on his jeans and made his way to the bathroom, then headed into the kitchen for a drink of water.

"Are you all right?"

He jerked around, nearly spilling the water at the sound of Sarita's voice. She was standing in the doorway of the kitchen, wearing an old worn robe with her hair in wild disarray. He didn't think he'd ever seen a woman look more sensually appealing...even more appealing than the daydream he'd had earlier. "I just needed a drink."

Sarita wished now that she'd stayed in bed. But when she'd heard him up roaming around, the need to check on him, to make certain he was not ill, had been too strong to deny. Or maybe she'd just wanted to see him. A definite mistake! Standing here in only jeans, he looked more virile than any man had a right to look. "I just thought I should check to make certain you weren't ill," she said stiffly, trying to keep her gaze from traveling from his face to the rugged expanse of his chest.

"I appreciate the concern." The urge to stride across the room and pull her into his embrace was almost too strong to resist. His hand tightened around the edge of the counter to keep him from acting on the impulse.

She told herself to turn and leave, but instead her attention had been drawn to the scars that marred his shoulders and traveled downward. "Those must have hurt. Did you get them in the crash?"

He was fairly certain she wasn't wearing anything under that robe. "Yeah, but I must have been in shock or too cold to feel any pain. At least, at first." Trying not to think about how delicious she looked, he turned his mind back to that fateful day. "As I told you before, my memories are vague. I woke up in a snowdrift. The plane was a smoldering ruin. I remember being thrown forward and hitting something hard. The gashes on my shoulders and chest convinced me I'd been thrown out the front windshield."

Her hand fastened around the doorjamb keeping her from approaching and tracing the lines of injury with her fingers. "It's amazing that you survived. You said an old woodsman found you?"

He nodded. "I started off through the woods looking for help. It seemed like I went for hours. I remember falling and rolling a long way down. The next thing I knew I was in a cabin with an old trapper and he was making me drink some ungodly herbal tea, and my injures were plastered with some concoction he'd learned from the Eskimos."

When she thought of how his life had been left in the hands of an untrained old man, a chill raced through her. "Why didn't he contact the authorities and get you to a hospital?"

"Joe and the authorities didn't get along. That was why he lived so far out in the wilds—no one knew where to find him and he wanted to keep it that way. So he fixed me up the best he knew how. Lucky for me, his remedies worked."

Sarita recalled the day she'd heard the news that he'd died. She'd felt as if she'd been kicked in the stomach. She'd reasoned that her reaction was due to the fact that someone her age had died. Now she admitted that the impact had hit her harder than if Wolf had merely been someone who had died too young. He had meant something to her. Maybe he was right about her regretting the loose ends between them...the unspoken thank-yous. "I'm glad, too," she said.

His smile warmed. "And I'm glad you're glad."

The protectiveness she'd been experiencing toward him suddenly invaded her once again, and a worry that had been nagging at the back of her mind flew to the forefront. *Fair's fair,* she told herself. "Since you've felt so free to involve yourself in my dating choices, I'd just like to say that I hope you were honest when you said you were being cautious about getting emotionally involved with Janice."

"I have no intention of getting emotionally involved with her. I don't trust her."

Sarita smiled with relief. "Smart man."

The smile was enticing. Again Wolf wanted to cross the room and draw her into his arms. Again reason prevailed. They had barely stepped onto the threshold of being friends, and a bed in the stable with a black eye was not the way he wanted to spend the rest of the night. "I like to think I am." Deciding that he'd better retreat before the growing lust he was experiencing got any stronger, he headed toward the door. Three paces from her he stopped. She hadn't moved.

Sarita had ordered her legs to carry her out of his way, allowing him passage through the door. Instead she stood rooted, fascinated into inaction by the virile look of him.

Wolf saw the nervous flicker of her eyelids. He saw something else, too. He saw a heat in those dark depths that matched his own. Maybe he'd misjudged what would happen if he kissed her.

He took a step closer. Still she did not move. He reached out and traced the line of her jaw with his fingers.

Fire swept through Sarita, and her knees weakened. She couldn't move if she wanted to now.

Wolf's gaze focused on her lips. They looked so full, so warm, so soft, so inviting. Suddenly he was remembering Luis's challenge to him and Pike. This truce between him and Sarita was still very fragile. If he made a play for her now and she later found out he'd made an offer for the land and that her grandfather had countered with a scheme to nab her a husband, she would never trust him. And he wanted her trust. Until this moment he hadn't realized just how important that was to him. "We'd better get back to bed and get some sleep," he said gruffly. He captured her by the shoulders and gently lifted her out of his way. Then, planting a light kiss on her forehead, he added, "Good night, my newfound friend," and headed down the hall.

Sarita stood frozen, still unable to move. The imprint of his hands remained so intense, it was as if he was still holding her. Dizziness threatened and, realizing she was holding her breath, she gasped in air. That

brought her out of her immobility, and she sank against
the wall, seeking support for her weakened legs.

These lusty feelings Wolf was evoking in her could
only lead to trouble for both of them, she chided herself. Like her grandfather had said, they seemed to be
natural-born antagonists. The truce between them was
constantly wavering. Only hours ago at the café, she'd
wanted to give him a swift kick in the shins. The truce
was certain to break if they got too close, and Wolf
knew that. So, he'd set the boundaries for their relationship. He'd declared them friends, nothing more.
And she would abide by those rules.

Chapter Eight

Sarita's gaze traveled over her image in the mirror. It was nearly time for Greg to arrive for their date. The restaurant he'd chosen was one of the most exclusive in Phoenix. When he'd called to check with her to make certain his choice was acceptable to her, she'd known he was worried that she might not have appropriate attire. He'd even offered to take her someplace more casual. But she'd always wanted to dine at the Velvet Palate.

It had been a long time since she'd had reason to wear her simple, black cocktail dress but it still fit nicely. Demure but barely knee length and formfitting, it had a neckline that plunged just low enough to show a subtle bit of cleavage. Sheer silk stockings showed off her nicely shaped legs, and back stiletto heels added a definite touch of glamour. A simple pearl necklace, pearl earnings and a small black purse finished the ensemble.

As for her hair, Gladys had plaited it into a French

braid weaving a couple of pale pink ribbons into the tresses for just a touch of color. Sarita had finished her preparations by using a modest amount of makeup, going for the natural look. "You'll pass muster," she declared, and strode out of her room.

In the living room Wolf heard the tapping of her heels on the hardwood floor as she came down the hall. He, too, was dressed for the evening in a new suit, tie and boots. When he'd found out through Luis where Pike was taking Sarita, he'd paid extra to have the suit altered in time for this evening. He wasn't certain what he thought he could accomplish, but he refused to allow her to spend an entire evening with Pike without him being there to keep an eye on them. Silently he fumed at Luis who was clearly enjoying Sarita's newfound popularity.

Hoping she'd look too drab for Pike to continue with this charade or that her attire would not be up to Pike's standards and he'd be too embarrassed to take her to the Velvet Palate thus allowing her to see how shallow the man was, Wolf turned as she entered.

Damn! he cursed silently. She had definitely cleaned up well. She looked great. Any man who wouldn't want to show her off would be an idiot.

Sarita held back a gasp at the sight of the cowboy in front of her. He looked as sexy in a suit as he had in the kitchen a couple of nights ago, wearing nothing but his jeans. The thought of having him as a dance partner caused embers to spark and as the image became clearer, the embers flamed into a fire so hot her lust threatened to take her breath away.

"You look nice," Wolf said, hiding his reaction behind a mask of polite friendliness.

"You, too," she replied, jerking her gaze away and

feigning an interest in checking the contents of her purse. Something that felt very much like jealousy swirled through her. "Are you taking Janice out?"

"Claudia and Bradford. We're going to the Velvet Palate." He'd considered showing up there without any warning, but decided to announce it, then act as if he had no prior knowledge that that was her destination as well.

She eyed him suspiciously. "Really? That's where Greg is taking me." She was certain he was going there to spy on her. Normally she would have been angry, but instead she found herself feeling flattered.

"No kidding?" He shrugged. "Well, according to Claudia, it is considered *the* place in Phoenix. She nagged at me incessantly until I agreed to take her there." He made a mental note to brief his kid sister on this little white lie.

Disappointment that she'd been wrong and she really wasn't the reason for his choice of restaurants flowed through Sarita. "Well, I guess I'll be seeing you there," she said, then headed into the kitchen. Through the window she saw the silver Mercedes convertible Wolf had just purchased. Suddenly she was visualizing herself riding beside him in those plush leather seats.

A self-mocking smile curled one corner of her mouth. When the dust settled, truth would prevail. He was staying at this ranch and he looked as if he fitted in well here, but she and Luis weren't really in his social class. The Mercedes was his first step back from the wilds of Canada. The rest, she guessed, would come quickly. By the end of next week he'd probably have found a much more appropriate place to board until his new home was built.

Having used rational thought to dampen the lust he'd

provoked in her, she was certain she was once more in control of herself. Returning to the living room, she discovered him still there. This time instead of paying attention to the fit of the suit he was wearing, she took in the design and fabric. It was definitely expensive. Probably cost more than her wardrobe and Luis's combined. The boots probably cost even more.

"Is something wrong?" Wolf asked, breaking into her thoughts.

She looked up at his face to find him watching her with a frown. "No."

"The way you were staring at me made me feel as if I had a third eye in the middle of my forehead," he elaborated. Worried that she hadn't bought his lie about Claudia being the reason he'd chosen the Velvet Palate and that her anger toward him was building, he said, "I hope you're not upset that I'm going to be at the same restaurant. If you are, I promise I'll keep my back to you the entire evening. You can pretend I'm not even there. I'd offer to change my reservations but I don't want to disappoint Claudia, she's only here for a short while on fall break."

"No, your being there won't bother me," she assured him. His taking his kid sister to the kind of restaurant Sarita would have to save a year to go to was yet another example of how different their worlds were. And even though she knew that Wolf O'Malley could never be more than a friend, and that even a friendship between them would most likely end once he rejoined society, she couldn't help but think about how good he looked. Again wanting to escape his company, she went out onto the front porch to wait for Greg's arrival.

"Both you and Wolf are looking very good tonight," Luis remarked as she joined him.

"Thanks." Wishing Wolf didn't look so damn attractive, she let a touch of angry frustration escape in her voice.

Luis glanced at her. "You don't sound very happy about that."

"I'm just a little tense about socializing with the elite." This wasn't entirely a lie. The thought that she was going to be out of her element had been nagging at her all day.

Luis patted her hand. "You are as good as any of them."

"I know that. But sometimes I feel like someone needs to tell them."

Luis laughed. "I don't think you're going to have the least bit of trouble fitting in tonight. You are *chula*...beautiful, spicy and elegant."

Sarita couldn't stop herself from laughing. "You do know how to lift a girl's spirits."

He patted her hand again and returned to his whittling.

Sarita tried to relax. *Think of this as an adventure,* she told herself. Suddenly in her mind's eye she again saw herself and Wolf in Wolf's Mercedes. *Wrong date!* She switched Wolf to Greg. The excitement the first image had stirred was missing.

Seeing Greg's blue Porsche turn off the main road and come down their drive, she breathed a sigh of relief. At least the waiting part was over.

Wolf stepped out on the porch as Greg climbed out of his car. Noting the glance between the two men, Sarita had the impression of being caught in the middle of a battle. Not wanting to start the date off on a sour note, she gave Luis a quick kiss on the cheek, then met

Greg before he reached the porch. "Shall we get going," she suggested.

"Before big brother threatens to beat me to a pulp again?" Greg asked with a laugh. "Yes, I think that would be a good idea." He nodded toward the men on the porch. "Evening, Luis. Evening, O'Malley." Then, taking her arm, he guided her to his car and opened the door for her.

Once behind the wheel, he let out a low whistle. "You're looking very hot tonight. I'm going to be the envy of every man in the restaurant."

Sarita found herself beginning to enjoy this evening. "I haven't heard so much flattery since the night of my senior prom when my father and grandfather saw me in formal attire for the first time."

"You should dress up more often." Abruptly he frowned at himself. "Forget that. Now that I've discovered the woman behind the apron, I want to keep her to myself. You start dressing like this more often, and there'll be a line at your door."

The image of Greg as a used-car salesman popped into her mind. "You're spreading that a little too thick, don't you think?"

"You wouldn't say that if you were in my shoes," he retorted. His voice took on an inquisitive note. "Speaking of shoes or rather boots…looked like O'Malley was planning on going out tonight. Heard he was seeing Janice."

Sarita bit back the impulse to declare that Wolf was too smart to be attracted to Janice. In spite of his assurance that he was, she couldn't be certain of that. Janice had a great many attributes that could be used to break down any man's resistance and she knew how to use them. The thought of Wolf succumbing to Janice's charms caused Sarita's stomach to knot and she pushed it out of her mind. "He's taking his sister and Bradford to dinner tonight."

"Obviously not someplace in our little town." Suspicion spread over Greg's features. "I'll bet he's taking them to the Velvet Palate. He probably found out that's where we're going. It'd be just like him to try to ruin our evening." Greg reached for the phone. "I'll take you there another night. I know a much more romantic spot for tonight."

Sarita was amazed by how much she disliked that idea. She should have been happy to be away from Wolf's presence. Instead, she heard herself saying, "But I really want to go to the Velvet Palate. If they show up we can ignore them." She was even more amazed when she added a lie. "Besides, we don't know for certain they're even going to be there."

Greg put down the phone and smiled patronizingly. "You're right. The Velvet Palate is no place to take a child and an old man." He gently stroked her cheek. "I just want to ensure that I have you to myself."

"I'm your date." His touch had done nothing except cause her jaw to itch. She wanted to scratch it but, knowing that would be impolite, she clasped her hands tightly in her lap.

As a silence fell between them, she contemplated what she'd just done. She knew she wasn't afraid of being alone with Greg, so she should have been pleased with a change in plan that wouldn't have Wolf hovering in the background all evening.

Maybe, in the back of her mind, she was worried Greg would turn into an octopus…all hands and arms…and she would want an easy ride home. In which case she was using Wolf O'Malley as a safety net. If so, that was a peculiar turn of events. In fact, it was close to laughable considering their past.

"You have a very bemused expression on your face," Greg noted.

"I was just thinking how, in a million years, I would never have expected this evening to be happening."

"My clients have taught me that life takes some odd twists and turns."

She glanced at him. "I'm not certain I like being referred to as an *odd* twist."

He cast her a warm smile. "You are an unexpected, exciting, very pleasurable twist of fate."

She still didn't trust him, but he did make her feel desirable. "And you have a very nice way with words."

"I'm just being honest."

She stared out at the road ahead. He sounded sincere. Could she be misjudging him? Ever since Wolf returned from the dead, the world had seemed a bit out of kilter…sort of like experiencing weird, full-moon effects without the full moon.

"What kind of music do you prefer?" He opened a compartment between them, displaying a rack of CDs.

"I have eclectic taste," she replied.

"Then put the first one in. It's classical. I like driving to it."

Following his instructions, she started the music, then grateful she didn't have to search for subjects to make small talk with, settled into her seat to enjoy the rest of the drive. But instead of Greg, the music or the passing landscape occupying her thoughts, it was the image of a silver Mercedes speeding along behind them. *This preoccupation with Wolf O'Malley isn't healthy or smart!* She forced her mind to concentrate on the music and the scenery. Still, that silver Mercedes lingered in the recesses as if hidden by a twist in the road but still present.

A sense of adventure swept through her as they pulled up in front of the restaurant and the doorman opened her door for her. If Greg hadn't asked her out, she would probably never have set foot over the threshold of this place, she thought as he dropped his keys into the parking valet's hands, then joined her.

Inside, it was even more elegant than she'd imagined. The crystal sparkled. The silver glistened. A ten-piece orchestra filled one wall, and the dance floor was large enough for several couples. And yet the atmosphere was cozy. It was the candlelight, she decided. The chandeliers were dimmed, and flowers, along with oil candles of various shapes and sizes, provided romantic centerpieces for each table.

"Nice place," she said after they'd been seated and left to peruse the menu.

"The chef is excellent."

"Everything looks so good." The urge to see if Wolf was arriving was strong, but her back was toward the entrance, giving her no covert way of glancing in that direction.

At Greg's suggestion, they selected appetizers and a wine to go along with them, but waited to order their main course until after they'd had a little more time to read through the menu.

As the minutes ticked by incredibly slowly, she began to doubt that Wolf would actually show up. *He's probably had second thoughts about being at the same restaurant as Greg and me,* she mused and the glow of excitement she'd experienced when they arrived began to fade. Even trying to perk it back up by letting her gaze travel over her plush surroundings didn't work.

The realization that it had been the expectation of Wolf's presence that had given the spark to her evening caused a rush of frustration. The emotions he stirred in her had the flavor of romance. Her mind flashed back to the early-morning hours when he'd declared his friendship, making it clear he felt nothing more. Still she could not get the image of him looking so very virile out of her mind.

Falling for him belongs in the same category as eating a whole box of chocolates. The aftereffect could be devastating, she admitted to herself.

"Ya-hoo. Sarita." Greg tapped on her menu.

Startled, she looked over the top at him.

"You've been staring at the menu for a good five minutes. When I asked if you'd found anything that interested you, you made no response. I was wondering if you'd gotten so bored with my company you'd fallen asleep."

Realizing how totally she'd allowed Wolf to occupy her mind, she flushed. "No, I'm not bored. I'm just having a hard time deciding. Everything sounds so elegant," she lied.

Understanding suddenly showed on his face. "If you're concerned about the prices, forget them."

Sarita, who had until now not even really begun to read the menu, focused on it and her eyebrows rose. The prices were double and triple the most expensive places she'd ever gone to before. "Are you sure?"

Satisfied that he'd guessed rightly about what had been bothering her, he smiled. "I chose this place, remember? The food is well worth the cost."

She eyed the menu dubiously. "If you say so."

"I do. And I highly recommend the quail or the lobster tail."

"The quail," she said, trying not to let Wolf's absence put a damper on her evening.

The waiter had arrived with their appetizers, poured their wine and was taking their dinner order when a prickling on the back of her neck sent a current of renewed excitement through her.

"I can't believe it. I'm certain he followed us here," Greg growled, looking past her shoulder to the door.

Sarita feigned confusion. "Someone followed us here?" She raised an eyebrow in disbelief. "You can't mean Wolf O'Malley?"

"In the flesh."

Sarita glanced over her shoulder, and her heart began to pound faster. He'd come after all. Reminding herself that he'd had to pick up both his sister and Bradford, she realized that it had been her impatience that had caused her to expect him to arrive sooner. If he were a box of chocolates, she would be in serious danger of devouring the whole thing, she thought.

"Is there a problem, sir?" the waiter asked with concern, also looking toward the door as if worried that a brawl might break out at any moment.

Schooling an indifferent expression onto her face and a nonchalance into her voice, Sarita turned back to the waiter. "No, there's no problem."

"Just make certain the maître d' seats the threesome that just arrived on the other side of the room," Greg said, producing a hundred-dollar bill and extending it toward the waiter.

"Too late, sir," the man replied, eyeing the bill with true remorse.

Again Sarita glanced over her shoulder, this time to

see the maître d' leading Wolf and his party in their
direction. But before they reached the table where she
and Greg sat, the man seated them a few tables away.
"I'm sure that distance will be adequate for us to forget
they're here," she said, as if their proximity meant
nothing to her.

"I suppose," Greg conceded grudgingly, pocketing
the hundred.

"And I think we should return our attention to ordering our dinner," she added.

Greg nodded and did as she suggested.

As the waiter walked away, Greg issued a low groan
of displeasure. "It would appear that at least one of
their trio is determined to interrupt our evening."

Again Sarita glanced over her shoulder. Wolf and
Bradford appeared to be engrossed in their menus.
Claudia, however, was heading their way.

"Isn't this just the neatest place. I'm so glad I insisted Wolf bring me here," she gushed, arriving at
their table. Turning to Greg with wide-eyed innocence,
she added apologetically, "My brother told me that I
shouldn't disturb your evening, but I thought it would
be impolite to not at least say hello."

"Hello," Greg replied, his tone holding dismissal.

Again Sarita fought a surge of disappointment at being reminded that Wolf had only chosen this place because of his sister. Down deep, she'd continued to hope
that he'd been lying and that she'd been the reason he
was here. *Even if that was the case, he would only be
playing his big-brother role*, she reminded herself
curtly. Casting Greg a "be polite" glance, she turned
to Claudia. "Yes, this place is *neat*, and it was very
nice of you to come over and say hello."

Claudia grinned widely at her. "Well, I guess I'd

better be getting back," she said, and was heading toward her table before either Greg or Sarita could say another word.

Sarita found herself thinking that she'd caught a glimmer of conspiratorial excitement in Claudia's eyes when the girl grinned at her. The thought that maybe this restaurant hadn't been Claudia's choice...maybe Wolf had enlisted his sister's aid to make it look that way...flashed through her mind. *Or more likely I'm beginning to slip into a fantasy world,* she mocked herself, again reminding herself that even if he had enlisted Claudia's help it was only because he wanted to watch over her and not because he was romantically interested in her.

"To us getting to know each other better," Greg said, raising his wineglass to her.

Picking up hers she clicked it to his and took a sip.

"Now tell me how you like those oysters." He coaxed her attention to the appetizer in front of her.

The array on her platter was that of six oysters, each baked with a different topping. She tried the first. "Excellent," she admitted.

He smiled with approval.

For the next few minutes they ate, sipped wine and exchanged remarks about their choices. Every once in a while Sarita thought she could detect a prickling on her neck as if Wolf was looking her way. But once, when she was certain Greg wouldn't notice, she glanced covertly toward the other table to discover him giving his attention to his companions. She was letting the man get way too far under her skin.

"How about a couple of turns around the dance floor to rebuild our appetites before the salads arrive," Greg suggested.

Glad for any excuse to escape finding something to talk about until their next course arrived, Sarita nearly bounded to her feet. "An excellent idea." But as they headed to the dance floor a surge of inadequacy caused her steps to falter. "I'm not a very good dancer," she confessed.

"I will enjoy any excuse to have my arms around you." Taking her hand, Greg pulled her gently onto the hardwood floor, then slipped his other arm around her waist. "Relax and let your body flow with the music."

Sarita tried to do as instructed, but almost immediately she stepped on his foot. Coming to an abrupt halt, she flushed with embarrassment. "I'm very out of practice," she said, starting to ease out of his arms with the intention of returning to their table.

His hold tightened slightly. "Don't be a quitter. I'll keep it simple...two steps forward, one step back and no quick turns."

A part of her wanted to be a quitter, but returning to the table and making small talk was less appealing than stumbling around on the dance floor. "All right," she agreed. "It's your toes that are in danger."

He laughed gently and began to guide her to the music once again, counting quietly in her ear as they moved. His breath tickled her skin, and she had to fight the urge to scratch. Again she was tempted to end their dance, when she realized that she could see Wolf over Greg's shoulder. Immediately any desire to leave the dance floor vanished. The sight of him caused her heart to beat faster. He looked her way and, even though there was a room between them, she could feel the intensity of his dark gaze. Forgetting Greg, she imagined herself in Wolf's embrace.

"You're doing much better," Greg whispered in her ear.

"You're a good teacher," she lied, knowing it was the thought of dancing with Wolf that had melted her tension, allowing her movements to become more fluid. Her inner voice mocked her for such silliness. As long as it remained in her mind and went no further, what harm could a little imagining do? she argued, and allowed the fantasy to continue.

Claudia studied her brother. "Why don't you cut in?" she coaxed.

Rebuking himself for letting his interest in the couple on the dance floor become so obvious, Wolf jerked his attention back to his two dinner companions. "I'm just here to make certain Pike doesn't take advantage of her. Not to interfere with their evening."

Claudia grinned wryly at Bradford. "If you believe that, I've got some stock in the Brooklyn Bridge I'd like to sell you."

Bradford frowned at Wolf. "I have to admit I am a little puzzled by your insistence that Greg is going to take advantage of Sarita. She's always struck me as being levelheaded and mature. I'm sure she can take care of herself."

"Greg Pike is a worm who'll do anything for—" Wolf stopped himself before he said *profit*. That would have raised questions he couldn't answer.

Claudia cast him an impatient grimace. "If you were going to say 'get a woman under the sheets,' you didn't have to stop because of me. I'm not totally naive."

That possibility was one Wolf had avoided considering. His stomach twisted at the image of Sarita giving herself to Pike. "Surely she'd be too smart to jump into bed with him on their first date," he growled.

"I hope so. I've always thought of her as being one of those sweet but saucy old-fashioned girls," Bradford said. "I'd hate to have that illusion destroyed. I have so few left."

Claudia was again studying her brother speculatively. "I still don't buy this guardian angel routine. You're in love with her, aren't you? Come on, admit it."

"I care about her as a friend." His words left the taste of a lie in his mouth. Maybe he was a little more fond...maybe a lot more fond...of Sarita than he was ready to confess. Inwardly he groaned. That was a complication he didn't need.

Sudden inspiration showed on Bradford's face. "You think Greg's lying about him, Preston and Katherine buying another piece of land. You think he's courting Sarita in order to sweet-talk her into convincing her grandfather to sell him their land."

"The cad!" Claudia snapped.

Bradford shook his head. "Sarita's too smart for that."

Claudia glanced toward the couple now leaving the dance floor and frowned. "I don't know," she said, returning her gaze to her dinner companions. "She is getting on in age, and there aren't very many prospects in Lost River. If she is feeling desperate enough, she might not want to see the truth."

"I suppose you could be right," Bradford conceded. "And from what I've seen of Greg Pike and women, he can be charming and does seem to be able to manipulate them."

The fact that they were voicing the same worries

nagging at Wolf, only made him more uncomfortable. The urge to tell Sarita the truth was strong, but, if he did, Pike would get the land and Wolf and Luis would incur Sarita's wrath. Again he silently cursed the old man.

"She needs our help," Claudia declared. Her face screwed into an expression of intense concentration. "The only solution is to find her a more suitable suitor." Her gaze again leveled on Wolf. "What about you? You could use a wife, and Sarita would be a lot better choice than Janice Corbett."

Wolf found himself tempted to take up the role of suitor, but Luis's deal held him back. "Courting a woman shouldn't be a game," he growled in frustration.

Claudia sighed. "You're right." Her eyes brightened. "But you could flirt with her a little. Make her see that she can be desirable to men other than Greg Pike." Her gaze swung to Bradford. "What do you think, Mr. Dillion?"

"I think that interfering in affairs of the heart can lead to a great deal of trouble," he replied. After a moment he paused and added, "However, while I cannot say Greg has ever behaved unethically, he does come very near the line. I'm not so sure I would want him courting any daughter of mine."

Too bad Luis Lopez doesn't have Bradford's good sense, Wolf fumed to himself.

Claudia's manner became that of one prepared to stage a campaign. "Then it's agreed, we must do something."

"We will remain at a distance and keep our eye on them. That is all," Wolf said sternly. "Now eat."

For a moment she looked as if she would protest,

then with a shrug that suggested she thought he was
wrong but would go along with him for now, she
turned her attention to the salad in front of her.

Wolf covertly glanced toward Sarita's table. He
could not see her face, but he could read Pike's expression. It was that of a man determined to charm his
date, and it appeared from the relaxed lines on Pike's
face that he was doing just that. Mentally, Wolf cursed.

"It would appear that one of us isn't following orders and eating," Claudia said to Bradford in a whisper
loud enough to carry to Wolf's ears.

Wolf looked to his sister to find her watching him
with a teasing smile that suggested she didn't believe
him when he said his interest in Sarita was nothing
more than friendship. He issued another silent groan.
There was no way to predict what a fifteen-year-old
female might do. He should never have involved her
in this.

Sarita took a bite of dessert. It was a luscious concoction of chocolate cake with a chocolate-mocha filling, covered with chocolate icing and topped with dark
chocolate roses. A raspberry sauce had been drizzled
across the plate to add a touch of color and elegance.

"If I eat this whole thing, I might burst." She sighed
exaggeratedly and took another bite. "But I can't resist
it."

Greg took a sip of his coffee, then rose. "We'll
dance between bites."

Sarita beamed. "The perfect solution." But as they
headed to the dance floor, she knew her motivation
wasn't the exercise; it was the thought of being able to
see Wolf once again.

So that Greg would not be suspicious, she allowed

him to hold her close, and rested her head against his cheek. This gave her a view over his shoulder. This preoccupation with Wolf O'Malley wasn't good, she warned herself. Still, the desire to see him was worse than any craving she'd ever experienced.

Watching Greg lead Sarita to the dance floor, Wolf tensed. When she melted into the man's arms, his agitation grew. Had Pike plied her with enough wine and charm that she was succumbing to him?

"Looks like the evening is going well for Mr. Pike," Claudia observed worriedly.

"They do appear to be getting along very well," Bradford agreed.

Wolf rose. "Perhaps I should have a word with her."

Claudia grinned and leaned toward Bradford as her brother strode away from the table. "Looks like he's changed his mind about us simply watching," she whispered gleefully.

"So it would appear," Bradford replied, watching their host's back with a thoughtful expression.

Seeing Wolf approach, Sarita felt a thrill of excitement. His expression was that of a man with a purpose as his gaze locked onto hers and held it.

She read anger in those dark eyes and guessed he was thinking she was being a fool and falling for Greg. Her jaw tensed with indignation. *Or, maybe he's jealous,* a tiny voice inside whispered hopefully. *Not likely,* a louder one responded. *He's merely playing big brother.* As he stepped on the dance floor, she stiffened in anticipation of a confrontation.

"Is something wrong?" Greg asked, loosening his hold so that he could see her face. The taut line of her jaw caused him to frown, but before he could inquire further, he felt a tap on his shoulder. When he realized Wolf was attempting to cut in, his frown turned to a glower. "Go away."

"That's not polite," Wolf replied, standing his ground.

Knowing how determined Wolf could be, and not wanting to cause a scene, Sarita smiled beseechingly at Greg. "I'm sure the music will end in a minute."

"I suppose if it's all right with Sarita," Greg conceded reluctantly, not disguising his ire.

"I'm sure Wolf won't bother us again." She eased herself out of Greg's embrace, her tone coaxing him to leave handling Wolf to her.

Greg gave Wolf a look that said he'd better not, as he allowed him to take his place.

"You look as if you're enjoying yourself," Wolf said, slipping his arm around her and beginning to guide her across the floor.

His touch ignited a fire so intense it momentarily locked her vocal cords. Not wanting him to guess the effect he was having on her, she lowered her gaze to his shoulder. Up this close, it appeared even broader and stronger, and her blood raced faster. *You have your pride. Don't let him know how he's affecting you!* she admonished herself. "I was," she managed, her fight for control causing the words to come out with stiff coldness.

Damn! Wolf cursed himself. His interference was angering her. That could work in Pike's favor. "Nice place," he said, fighting down the urge to again warn her that Pike was not a man to be trusted.

"Very," she conceded. The urge to move closer for a more intimate contact was strong.

She felt so soft beneath the hand he was pressing

against her back, Wolf found himself tempted to draw her closer. Even stronger was the urge to throw her over his shoulder and carry her out of here and take her home. Cutting in on her and Pike had been a very bad idea. "I'm glad you're having a nice time."

She looked at him then. The hard line of his jaw belied his words. "No, you're not," she said. Again the tiny spark of hope that he was jealous flared to life.

"You're right," he admitted gruffly. "I'm worried you'll fall for Pike's lies. For your sake I want you to move slowly where he's concerned."

Frustration raged through her. He was merely playing big brother. "I am not the kind of woman who behaves rashly, and I do not need you standing guard over me."

Provoking her was not what he'd wanted to do. "You're right. I apologize for interfering with your evening." Forcing himself to release her, he motioned for her to precede him off the dance floor.

Freed, she missed the warmth of his embrace. *He thinks of you as a friend, nothing more,* she fumed at herself. *And maybe not even a real friend,* she added. It could be that he simply considered her someone who needed strong guidance. That's how he'd seen her in their youth. Striding back to her table, she didn't look at him once.

"Thanks for the dance," he said, holding her chair for her as Greg rose at their approach.

"You're welcome," she returned stiffly, still refusing to look his way.

"It would appear that O'Malley ticked you off," Greg observed. Reaching across the table, he took her hand in his. "I should never have left you alone with him. He can be a real irritant."

Inwardly she continued to fume. It wasn't Wolf who had made her mad, it was herself and the way her body had wanted to remain in Wolf's arms. *Forget the man!* she ordered herself and forced a smile for Greg. "I refuse to let him ruin my evening," she said. Her gaze lowered to the dessert in front of her. "He falls into the category of sour lemon balls. I prefer to concentrate on the sweeter things in life."

"I can be very sweet," Greg assured her.

She forced a playful smile. "I'm sure you can." Freeing her hand, she took a bite of the dessert. It tasted dull. Glancing around the room, she realized that their surroundings no longer pleased her, either, and she wished the evening would end.

And it finally had. Sarita slipped on her nightgown, then sat down on the window seat in her bedroom and began to brush her hair. As soon as they'd finished dessert, Greg had suggested they leave the restaurant. Once in the car, he'd wanted to take her to a comedy club, but she'd pleaded a headache and asked to be brought home.

With the perfect amount of concern mingled with regret, he'd complied. At her door he'd kissed her lightly and asked her to come to a dance at the country club the following Saturday. She'd considered refusing, then recalling the disturbing effect Wolf was having on her, she decided that staying at home alone would not help, and accepted Greg's invitation. Now she was having second thoughts. She was used to waiting on the people who belonged to the country club, not socializing with them.

She frowned at herself. That wasn't the real reason she was considering backing out of the date. She simply didn't enjoy Greg's company. He was pleasant, charming, flattering, attentive…all the things a date should be. She just didn't trust him. Dating her was out of character and she couldn't shake the feeling that he had an ulterior motive. He could very easily be lying about buying land elsewhere and still be after her grandfather's property. This wasn't a flattering thought, but, knowing Greg, Katherine and Preston, it was certainly a possibility.

Leaning back, she closed her eyes. Immediately Wolf's image filled her mind. *Get that man out of your head,* she screamed at herself in frustration.

But no sooner had she vanquished him than she heard his car coming down the drive, and once again he captured her attention. Guided by the sound of his movements, in her mind's eye, she saw him entering the house, passing through the kitchen and coming down the hall. At her door he hesitated, and she held her breath wondering if he was going to knock. He didn't, but instead, continued to his room.

A short while later she heard the shower running and visualized him under the cascade of water…the broad expanse of his shoulders…the hard musculature of his abdomen. Those required no imagination, she'd seen them. But her mind didn't stop there. With a depth of imagination she hadn't known she had where men were concerned, her musing became more intimate until the fires his touch on the dance floor had stoked to life again burned hot.

Get a grip on yourself, she ordered when she realized her breathing was becoming irregular and desire had become a burning core within her. Jerking herself to her feet, she again vanquished his image.

Feeling too confined in her room, she pulled on her

robe and went out on the front porch. The night air smelled comforting. Seating herself in the rocker, she propped her slippered feet on the rail and gazed out at the stars. Before Wolf's return, her life had been comfortable. *Dull,* her inner voice corrected.

She shifted restlessly. Hearing the whinny of a horse, she thought of her mare and Thunder and wondered if they were having a nice little frolic together. The thought that she'd like to be having a frolic in the hay with someone flashed into her mind and she breathed a harsh sigh of frustration as the image of the partner she had in mind came into focus. It was Wolf.

"Evening." A male voice broke the stillness of the night.

She stiffened as Wolf came out on the porch and leaned against the post in her line of vision. To her relief he'd pulled on a shirt along with his jeans. "Evening."

"Appears you beat me home. Pike get fresh?" He pictured himself punching the guy if he'd done anything to hurt Sarita.

"No. He got boring," she confessed.

Wolf smiled. "So you're not going to be seeing him again."

She frowned at the night sky. "Actually, I am. He invited me to a dance at the country club next Saturday night, and I accepted."

Wolf's smile turned to a scowl. "If he bores you, then why go out with him?"

Her gaze swung to him. "Because he asked, and I'm tired of sitting at home alone."

Wolf didn't like the sound of that. A woman, bored and feeling alone, was an open invitation to an opportunist, and Greg Pike was an opportunist. "I'm sure you could find someone a hell of a lot more suitable than him for a companion.''

''I don't see anyone else beating a path to my door.''

A curl of fear wove through Wolf. She looked vulnerable...too vulnerable. He couldn't stomach the thought of her with Pike. Reaching her in one stride, he cupped her face in his hands. Her skin beneath his palms was soft and enticing, igniting a fire within him. ''Don't do anything rash. You'll regret it.''

His touch was like a warm blanket, and she saw a heat building in his eyes. ''A person has to take a chance once in their lifetime,'' she said, her body craving the opportunity to take that chance with him.

She looked incredibly kissable. Again he pictured her with Pike. ''Not with Pike,'' he growled.

''No, not with Pike,'' she replied.

He heard the invitation in her voice, and the desire to accept it was close to overwhelming. But he knew her well enough to know how she'd react when she found out about the challenge Luis had issued. She'd be furious, and he'd lose her trust. First thing tomorrow morning he was going to have a stern talk with Luis. The man had to call the challenge off. Releasing her abruptly, he straightened. ''It's late, we'd better get some sleep.''

Idiot! Fool! she mocked herself as he disappeared inside. She'd made a pass at him, and he'd turned tail and run as fast as he could. Even though a physical attraction was there, he was clearly determined to keep his distance. How could she have done something so ridiculous? Embarrassment brought a flush to her skin.

She wanted to stamp her feet and let out a shriek of

frustration. Instead, she settled for going inside and going to bed. But sleep didn't come easy, and when it did, Wolf haunted her dreams...mocking her attempt to flirt with him.

Chapter Nine

Wolf arrived at church early the next morning. Afraid that, out of frustration and anger, he might say something to Luis in front of Sarita that would cause her to guess Luis's game, he'd left the house as quickly as possible. He wouldn't be the cause of Pike gaining what he wanted and Sarita having her dignity injured, all with one slip of the tongue. Even more, from the conversation he'd overheard between her and her grandfather on his first day back, he recalled her saying that the land was as much a part of her as it was of Luis. His jaw hardened with purpose. He had to find a way out of this mess that would not cause her to lose anything she held dear.

Entering the sanctuary, he chose a seat at the far end of the rear pew. From there he could see both friend and foe with ease. As the church began to fill, Katherine entered with Preston and Claudia. He saw his sister spot him. Immediately she gave her mother's arm a tug and said something to her. Wolf guessed she was asking Katherine if she could sit with him. When Claudia parted company with her mother and Preston and headed in his direction, he knew he was right. He also noted that neither Katherine nor Preston even looked his way. Both were clearly intent on ignoring his presence.

"Good morning," Claudia said happily, slipping into the pew beside him.

"Morning."

She leaned conspiratorially toward him. "This is so great. Mother thinks she can use me to spy on you, so she's letting me spend as much time as possible with you."

That his sister had seen through her mother's game, pleased him. "Sometimes good can come out of even one of Katherine's ploys."

Claudia grinned her agreement, then asked, "What time did Sarita get home?"

"She was there when I arrived." Again he recalled his relief when he'd gone out on the porch and discovered her there in her robe and realized that even though he'd heard nothing in her room when he'd arrived home, she'd been there.

"That's great. That means the date didn't go as well as Mr. Pike had planned."

Wolf recalled the hurt of rejection he'd seen in Sarita's eyes when he had not accepted her invitation to kiss her and he knew the extent of her pride. "I may have helped his cause," he admitted grimly.

Claudia looked stricken. "You didn't. Tell me you didn't." When Wolf made no response, she frowned at him with indulgent reprimand. "All right, what did you do?"

"I didn't kiss her," he growled. Even now he could

still recall how delicious her lips had looked and how it had taken every ounce of his strength not to give in to the impulse to take her into his arms.

Claudia's eyes rounded. "Kiss her?"

"It's a long story." His tone let her know he didn't want to tell it.

For a long moment she simply continued to frown at him, clearly hoping her disapproval would cause him to elaborate. When that didn't work, she said, "Daddy always said you were a man of principle but I can't believe you would harm our plan to save her because of a little kiss. Men go around kissing women they don't love all the time."

It pleased him to know that his father had considered him a man of principle. There had been times when he'd wondered if Katherine had managed to plant doubt about that in his father's mind, as well. Apparently she hadn't. "Sarita is not a woman a man should play games with."

Claudia sighed. "You're right. I wouldn't want a man to kiss me if he didn't mean it, even if it was for my own good." A new twinkle entered her eyes. "But she did want you to kiss her?"

"Who knows what a woman wants for sure," he said, hedging.

"I still think she would be a good match for you. And I'd love to have a couple of nieces and nephews. I'd even baby-sit for free," she coaxed.

The image of him and Sarita with a couple of children filled Wolf's mind. He liked it...he liked it a lot. What he didn't like was the look in his sister's eyes. It suggested that she might try a little matchmaking and, if Luis refused to see reason, that could cause more trouble than he already had. "I'll keep your suggestion in mind as long as you keep it our secret and let me handle this my way,'' he said.

Claudia smiled triumphantly. ''You've got a deal.''

Suddenly she nudged him hard, and he looked to the aisle to see that Sarita and Luis had arrived. The old man nodded in his direction, but Sarita acted as if he didn't exist as she continued to their usual pew.

''Wow, she really is angry with you,'' Claudia whispered.

Just like old times. Wolf hated this thought. He liked having Sarita to talk to. He especially liked having her on his side. Fervently he prayed that Luis would listen to reason.

Out of the corner of her eye, Sarita had seen Wolf's gaze turn to her. Inwardly she cringed, while outwardly she held her head high and ignored him. He'd nearly raced out of the house this morning, and she guessed by noon he'd have succeeded in finding new quarters.

Self-directed fury raged through her. Why hadn't she stayed in her room last night? And how could she have been so weak as to let Wolf see the attraction she was feeling? Because she'd thought he was feeling the same, her inner voice defended. She'd seen the heat in his eyes. But he'd recognized it for what it was…nothing but lust. And, while she'd been ready to give in to it, he'd had the honor and common sense to hold himself back. His friendship was all he was willing to offer her. Now she was embarrassed to face him, and he was uncomfortable around her.

A self-directed curse flew through her mind. Immediately remembering where she was, she quickly prayed for forgiveness.

"You look like a woman with a heavy load on her mind." Greg's voice interrupted her plea.

She glanced to the side to see him seating himself beside her. Surprise registered on her face.

"I hope you aren't saving this place for someone else," he said.

Sarita saw her own surprise reflected on the faces of several nearby parishioners. "No, I just didn't expect you to sit with us."

"I'm sitting with *you*," he corrected.

"Especially with me." More heads had turned in their direction, and some of the elderly women were whispering to each other behind their hands. "Sitting with a woman in church leads to all kinds of speculation—speculation that usually involves engagements and marriage."

He grinned. "I told you I was serious." Leaning around her, he extended his hand to Luis. "Good morning, sir. You have a lovely granddaughter."

"I think so," Luis replied with a proud smile.

Past Greg's shoulder, Sarita saw Wolf watching them. To most others his expression would have been unreadable, but she knew that look well. Behind it was controlled anger. Her chin tightened with defiance. Just because *he* didn't consider her good wife material didn't give him the right to think that every man who did had an ulterior motive. Giving Greg her full attention, she smiled warmly. "I had a nice time last night."

"I'm glad. I've been thinking that waiting until next Saturday to see you again is too long. How about a movie this evening?"

"Sure," she replied without hesitation. And, tonight she would concentrate on him. It could be that she'd misjudged him. Maybe he was honestly ready to settle down.

"I'll pick you up around six." He gave her hand a squeeze before reaching for a hymnbook.

His touch left her cold. A mental shriek of frustration echoed in her head.

Wolf's gaze traveled from one of his luncheon companions to the other. Sarita was determinedly ignoring him while Luis seemed perfectly at ease, enjoying his food as if all was well.

But all wasn't well. For Wolf, the silence at the table was deafening. "I thought the minister's sermon today was very good," he said.

Sarita had figured that he would. Reverend Brown had talked about prudence and the consequences of acting rashly. She simply cast Wolf a dry look and continued to eat.

"He's an old man. He lacks the adventure of youth," Luis said.

"Sometimes adventures can lead to trouble," Wolf countered.

"Better a little danger than to live out your life like a dried prune with no life in you," Luis replied.

Sarita had no doubt they were talking about her. "I don't think I like that last description," she grumbled.

Luis smiled. "Then it's up to you to make certain it doesn't fit you."

"I'm working on that. I have a date with Greg this evening." Unable to control her urge to let Wolf know that some men desired her company, she added, "He said he didn't want to wait until next Saturday to see me again."

Wolf could barely control his rage. Her grandfather

was encouraging her to follow a path that could prove hurtful, even destructive. "If you'll excuse me, I need some fresh air." Rising, he carried his plate to the sink, then strode out the back door.

At the corral housing Thunder and Sarita's mare, he leaned on the railing and frowned musingly at the stallion. "I envy you," he grumbled under his breath. "Life is so simple. You see a mare you like, you breed, that's the end of it. No tempers to deal with. No grandfathers playing games."

"Hi, cowboy." A female voice interrupted. "Since you wouldn't come see me, I decided I'd come pay you a call. I'll admit, it's a little hard on my ego, but then you've always been a difficult man."

Wolf turned to see Janice approaching. She was wearing a low-cut, red sundress that showed off all her features. His first reaction was to mentally groan. She was the last person he'd wanted to see. Then it dawned on him that she might have information he wanted. "Afternoon."

"I have located a three-year-old stallion you might be interested in. Even if you breed Thunder successfully, it'll be a long time before you have a horse to ride. Also, the same man has a gentle mare. Since you seem to be spending so much time with Claudia, I thought you might be in the market for a ride for her." Reaching him, Janice aimed a kiss at his mouth, but Wolf turned his head, causing it to land on his cheek. She rewarded him with a petulant pout. "I spent hours locating those horses. I should have some reward."

"You have my sincere gratitude for your effort."

She sighed. "I suppose I'll have to settle for that."

Keeping his tone conversational, Wolf said, "Have you heard about Greg Pike courting Sarita?"

Janice's eyes glistened with amusement. "Who hasn't. Especially after this morning when he sat with her in church. Around here that's practically an announcement of an engagement. People are already speculating on the wedding date and how long the marriage will last. Most give it less than two years. Greg is not the settling-down type, and Sarita doesn't strike me as the kind of woman who'd put up with a philandering husband."

"My thoughts, too." He fought to keep his tone casual. "So you think Pike will actually marry her?"

Janice lowered her voice. "I know he will. He wants the canyon."

Wolf raised an eyebrow questioningly.

"Katherine told me about the deal Luis offered."

Wolf allowed his surprise to show. "Katherine doesn't like her confidantes divulging information."

Janice flicked a shoulder in a who-cares manner. "She made me mad. She suggested I'd lost my ability to wrap men around my little finger. She won't accept the fact that you're one of those men who won't be wrapped around any woman's little finger."

Thank goodness for Janice's vanity, Wolf thought. "I still find it difficult to believe that even Pike would marry for a bit of land. There have to be other suitable sites for the spa they want to build."

"You'd think so," Janice agreed. "But apparently they have their heart set on the canyon. You know Katherine—once she gets an idea into her head even a stampede of wild horses can't run it out."

"Sometimes I wonder if that woman isn't a few horses short of a full herd," Wolf muttered.

Janice laughed. "If I ever forgive her, I won't mention you said that."

Deciding he'd learned all he could from Janice regarding Pike, Wolf changed the subject. "So where are those horses you think I might be interested in?"

"I'll take you there. We'll have a lovely afternoon looking over beautiful horseflesh." She reached for his arm.

Wolf avoided her grasp. "No." Mentally, he berated himself. That had come out too sharply. He might need her help in the future. "I'm not good company right now," he added apologetically. "Besides, I have something I have to do."

"Like save Sarita Lopez from your evil stepmother and her cohort." Janice frowned petulantly. "Too bad I'm not the one needing saving. I'd enjoy you riding in on your white charger to rescue me."

"It's not my stepmother and Pike I have to deal with," Wolf growled.

Janice's eyes sparkled with dislike. "Oh, yes. It's the grandfather, right? He's the one who is so worried she's going to end up a spinster, he's offered her for the canyon. I doubt you'll be able to talk him out of it. He's always struck me as being a little loco." Anger showed on her face. "And once he sets his mind on something, it can't be changed. Believe me, I know."

"He can be stubborn," Wolf conceded. "But he's not loco. He's just living in the past, when a woman was courted for her dowry. The problem is this isn't the past, and Sarita will be furious if she ever finds out the truth."

"Well, she won't find out from me. I might be willing to tell you what Katherine said, but I know what lines not to cross. If Katherine ever found out I spilled the beans to Sarita and cost her and Greg that canyon, she'd come after me with a vengeance, and Katherine's talons are not to be taken lightly."

"I know," Wolf replied.

A look passed between them that said they understood each other well on this point.

"So where do I find the horses?" Wolf asked again, a plan beginning to bud.

Janice gave him directions.

Inwardly Wolf smiled. The ranch was quite a distance away. Good thing he hadn't had time to contact Hank Jefferies about that horse Luis had suggested. "And now it'd be best if you went on your way," he said when she finished, his tone more an order than a request. "I've got a mess to untangle here, and if I do get it untangled, you don't want Katherine thinking you helped."

Janice breathed a regretful sigh. "You're right." Reaching up, she traced the line of his jaw with her finger. "When you get done trying to save your damsel in distress, give me a call."

Wolf's expression hardened. "I hope I can do more than just try. I'd hate to see Sarita fall victim to my stepmother and Pike."

Janice smiled. "That's the one thing I've always admired most about you. Others thought you were a pain in the neck, but you're like Don Quixote, always tilting at windmills...with Katherine being the biggest and most formidable. Of course, I will admit, I also thought you were taking the rough road for no real reason. You should have ignored her."

"She took my father from me and made me an outcast in my own home."

Janice gave him an encouraging look. "Good luck. You're going to need it." Then with her hips swaying enticingly, she strolled back to her car, paused to wave as she climbed in, then drove away.

Sarita had been watching the couple from the kitchen window. Jealousy curled through her. Silently she berated herself for feeling jealous about a man who had proven he was not the least bit romantically inclined toward her. Still, that he hadn't left with Janice or appeared to be following her pleased her.

When he started back toward the house, she quickly occupied herself with scrubbing the pans.

Wolf decided that when this was all over, he owed Janice a gift. She'd supplied him with a way to occupy Sarita's afternoon without appearing to be courting her. "I was wondering if you'd mind doing me a favor," he said as he entered the kitchen.

She started to give him a glare that said she couldn't believe he'd ask anything of her after his late-night rejection, but stopped herself. He had said he wanted to be her friend. If she refused to respect his request, she would appear small and petty. Even worse, he'd know how much his rejection had hurt her. "What favor?"

"Janice has located a couple of horses she thinks I might be interested in purchasing. I was hoping you would come take a look at them with me and give me your opinion."

Sarita could barely believe her ears. "You want my opinion about a couple of horses?"

"You know animals. You were even able to handle Thunder. Most people wouldn't have been able to."

"I didn't *handle* Thunder. I offered him sanctuary, and he was smart enough to take it."

Wolf used his second argument. "Another reason I'd like for you to come is that my stables aren't ready for occupancy just yet. Any horse I purchase, I'd like to be housed here for a while. But I wouldn't want to do that if you thought they wouldn't be compatible with your horses."

He was obviously determined to have her accompany him, and she could think of no polite way to get out of it. Looking for a bright side, she decided she could use this afternoon to heal her wounded pride. She would spend the time with him and show no sign that she retained any lingering attraction. That should convince him last night was a fluke, a momentary insanity, and would never happen again. "All right, I'll go with you. But we have to be home in time for me to get ready for my date with Greg."

"Sure, I'll have you home in plenty of time." Normally a man of his word, Wolf had no intention of keeping this commitment. Tomorrow when she was at work, he would talk with Luis. Tonight he'd make certain she didn't get home until it was too late for her to keep her date with Pike.

Sarita glanced at her watch. They'd been on the road for nearly two hours. From soon after they'd started this trek, she'd been angry with herself for agreeing to come. At first she'd tried to make small talk to show him that she was at ease but indifferent to his company. But making small talk didn't come naturally. Realizing she was simply rattling on and beginning to sound inane, she'd shut up. And Wolf had seemed happy to ride in silence. So for the past hour and a half they'd barely spoken two words, and she'd had only music to soothe her taut nerves. "I thought you said Janice said the ranch was less than an hour's drive."

Wolf glanced around at the barren landscape. He

knew his reticence was annoying her, but he was afraid of what he might say if they started talking. He couldn't keep his mind off Pike. "I must have taken a wrong turn somewhere."

"Obviously," Sarita returned dryly.

He schooled apology into his features. "I've been away a long time. When Janice was giving me directions I was certain I knew where I was going. Guess I got a little confused."

He looked so repentant Sarita experienced a twinge of guilt at being so critical. "There was a gas station about five miles back. Why don't we go back there and ask directions?"

"With a little backtracking, I'm sure I can get us to the ranch."

She scowled at him. "Why is it that men always refuse to ask directions? You'd rather drive around for hours before admitting you're lost. Is it some ego thing?"

"We're not lost. We're simply not where we intended to be."

She raised an eyebrow skeptically. "We're not lost?"

"We're west of Phoenix and east of the Arizona border."

She couldn't suppress a small chuckle. "I wouldn't be so certain about being east of the border."

Again Wolf found himself thinking that she looked incredibly kissable. The urge to pull over and act on that urge was close to overwhelming. Tightening his hands on the steering wheel, he concentrated on making a U-turn. "All right, we'll go back and ask directions."

"We're not going to have much time to inspect those

horses,'' Sarita warned, determined to remind him of her date with Greg.

"Don't worry," Wolf soothed.

She'd expected a hint of anger at the reminder. Instead there was a mellowness in his voice, and suspicion sparked to life. Was he playing big brother again? She eyed him covertly, but said nothing.

Twenty minutes later they pulled into the ranch they were seeking.

The owner, a man by the name of Red Parker, tall, lean, in his early forties, came out to greet them. "Thought you might have gotten lost," he said, extending his hand, first to Sarita and then to Wolf.

"We did," Sarita replied, her suspicion continuing to grow.

"I've got the horses saddled and ready to go." Red led them around the house toward the corrals as he spoke.

Sarita looked up at Wolf. "We're going for a ride?"

"You can't tell the metal of a horse just by looking at it."

She considered protesting, but stopped herself. Riding had always been a cure for her taut nerves. Besides, he was right. "A short ride," she stipulated.

"Certainly," he agreed.

Again she noted that he was much too amenable. Anger bubbled within her. He wasn't interested in her romantically but he wanted to control her love life. Well, he'd find out that she wasn't someone he could manipulate.

Reaching the horses, Wolf gave the mare and the stallion a thorough inspection before they mounted. Then with Red guiding them, they headed out onto the open land beyond the barns.

"Nice place you have here," Wolf addressed their host. "Fine horses, too."

Red smiled with pride. "I like to think so."

"I heard you had a herd of purebred mustangs that roam free on your land."

"They're yonder." Red nodded toward the west. "It's a bit of a ride."

"I'd like to see them. It'd give us a chance to give these horses a run," Wolf said.

"Won't be a short ride, even if we run 'em," Red warned.

Wolf turned in his saddle to face Sarita, again apology was etched into his features. "Do you mind? I'm thinking of getting a couple of mustangs to use for breeding stock. I've got a cell phone in the car. You can call Pike when we get back and warn him that you might be a little late. I'm sure he won't mind waiting."

Sarita knew she'd look petty if she refused. After all, they had come a long way. "As long as we're here, you might as well check out all of the horses," she replied.

Wolf had to fight to keep triumph from showing. "Thanks. You're a real friend."

Friend. The word stung. Furious with herself for still wanting more than that from him, she said curtly, "I thought we were going to run these horses."

Wolf gave Red a nod, and they kicked their mounts into a gallop.

The sun was low on the horizon by the time they returned to the ranch house.

"It's going to take a bit more time for the paperwork," Wolf warned her. "If you're as impressed with these horses as I am, I'm going to purchase them."

"They're fine animals," she conceded, giving her mare a friendly pat and rub. The hard riding and her stressed-out nerves had tired her. Too exhausted to be angry with him, she was willing to concede that for today he'd won his objective. It was too late for her to make her date with Greg. But, she vowed, she wouldn't allow him to manipulate her this way again.

"And I'd like a couple of those mustangs, too," Wolf added to Red as they headed to the house.

"I'll give Greg a call from your car phone and take a rain check on our date," she said, turning toward Wolf's car.

"Sorry this took so long," he apologized, again fighting to keep the innocence on his face and in his voice.

"I'll just bet you are," she returned.

"You can never be too careful when looking for good horses," Wolf said, ignoring the accusation in her voice.

Shaking her head, she continued on to the car. Did he think she was that naive?

Greg was not happy about her canceling their date. "I'll drive up there and pick you up," he offered.

She was flattered, but she also had to admit that she wasn't that interested in seeing him. "I'm not dressed for a date. I smell like horses, and my hair's a mess."

"I'm sure you look and smell perfectly charming," he persisted.

"We got so lost on our way up here, I don't even know for certain how long it will take you to get here and I can't give you decent directions. Besides, I'm exhausted. We ran the horses a great deal of the way, and then Wolf wanted to cut into the herd of mustangs. I haven't worked a horse so hard in years."

A sigh of resignation came over the line. "All right. But I'm taking you out to dinner and a movie tomorrow night. I want to see you again...soon."

Her gaze turned to the ranch house, where Wolf was consulting with Red, and she scowled. There was no future for her in there. She should give Greg a second look. "Tomorrow night," she agreed.

A while later as they drove home, Wolf said, "I appreciate your coming along."

"I'm not a fool, Wolf O'Malley," she snapped back. "I know you're playing big brother again and only did this to keep me from going out with Greg."

Deciding that piling one lie on top of another was not going to gain her trust, Wolf grimaced self-consciously. "He's not the right man for you."

Startled that he'd actually admitted this whole afternoon had been a ploy, she stared at him. "I can't believe you went so far as to get us lost just to keep me from keeping my date."

"We were never lost...just off track a little."

"I'd say you went a little above and beyond friendship." As soon as the words were out, her stomach knotted. She'd practically asked him if he was reconsidering his feelings for her.

Again Wolf had to fight the urge to tell her that what he was feeling definitely went beyond friendship. "I wasn't just keeping you from your date. I really do respect your opinion about horses," he said. "I honestly wanted you with me when I made my decision."

Respect and friendship was all he felt for her. Sarita hid her disappointment. "Then, at least, I didn't entirely waste my day," she said flippantly, pretending that her previous remark had been of no real significance. Then, settling back into her seat, she concentrated on the passing landscape.

Chapter Ten

Wolf had never thought he would ever consider throttling an elderly man, but at this moment his patience with Luis was reaching a serious breaking point. "You can't possibly want her to marry Pike. You know it won't last. The man has no staying power."

"For Sarita, he might change," Luis said with calm confidence.

"Can a leopard change his spots? Can a zebra change his stripes?" Wolf returned. "No. And Greg Pike isn't going to change, either."

"If you're so worried about her, you could marry her." Luis repeated the solution he'd suggested during their first confrontation on this matter.

"I've told you, I will not consider marrying her as long as there are strings attached. She's too strong willed. If she found out, and secrets are always found out in the end, she'd never trust me."

Luis shrugged. "Then you must do what you must do. I have given my word."

Realizing this was getting him nowhere, Wolf stormed out of the house.

He couldn't let her marry Pike. He couldn't stand for her to even be in the man's company. In his mind he replayed their late-night encounter in the kitchen and the one on the porch. He was certain he'd seen desire in her eyes…a desire as strong as his own. Or, at least, that's what he hoped he'd seen. Cursing Luis under his breath, he drove into town.

"So you really think you're going to be the one to get Greg Pike to settle down?" Vivian Kale asked when Sarita approached her table.

The cattiness in her voice let Sarita know the woman didn't believe she could. Earlier, upon her arrival at work, both Jules and Gladys had again expressed their concern that Greg wasn't the settling-down type. She hadn't minded their friendly concern. But Vivian wasn't being friendly. She was ridiculing Sarita for even considering the possibility Sarita could tame a man like Greg. She considered a snappy answer, then decided that would only make her look defensive. "I'm not even sure I want to try."

Looking shocked, Vivian's gaze raked over her. "I'd think you'd be flattered by his attention."

"I might be flattered, but I'm not naive," Sarita returned, then poised her pen with authority. "Are you ready to order?"

Vivian looked as if she was going to refuse to take the hint that their conversation regarding Greg was over.

"If you want more time, I'll come back in a few minutes," Sarita added before the woman could persist in her determination to interfere in Sarita's personal life. Starting to turn away, she caught a sparkle in Vivian's eyes, then saw Greg entering.

"And how is the loveliest waitress in town this morning?" he asked, heading toward her.

She saw several of the patrons grin.

"Looks like the man's serious," Charlie offered in a voice loud enough to carry across half the room.

Greg frowned as his gaze traveled over the assembly. "Of course I'm serious. I hope none of you have been suggesting otherwise."

On other occasions Sarita had heard him admonish others. But on those occasions there had always been a charming edge in his voice so that while he had admonished them, he had not offended them. She'd guessed he'd learned that subtle ability dealing with juries. Today, however, there was an undisguised threat in his voice, and she read the surprise on the faces of the other patrons.

Greg turned his attention back to her. "I hope one of your tables is open."

She nodded toward one against the wall. "You can sit there."

Greg had just started toward it, when the door was thrust open and Wolf entered. His expression grim, he strode to Sarita and captured her by the arm. "I want to talk to you. In private," he growled, guiding her toward the kitchen.

Greg grabbed Wolf's arm. "I'd appreciate it if you wouldn't manhandle my woman."

Wolf paused to glare at him. "She's *not* your woman." Jerking free from Greg's hold, he continued to guide Sarita toward the kitchen.

"The hell she isn't," Greg snapped, following on Wolf's heels.

At first, Sarita had been too startled to be embarrassed. Now a flush was beginning to build. "Let go of me," she demanded as he pushed open the door between the dining room and kitchen.

Wolf ignored the order, pulling her inside with him.

"What is the meaning of this?" Jules demanded, glowering threateningly at Wolf while holding up his spatula like a weapon ready to strike. "Release my waitress. I will not stand for her to be manhandled."

Gladys thrust the door open, nearly colliding with Greg's back as she too entered the kitchen. "What's going on?"

"I love Sarita, and I'm asking her to marry me," Wolf said bluntly. As he spoke the words, he knew he'd never wanted anything more. Fear that she would refuse swept through him. Vowing he wouldn't give up without a fight, his gaze bore into her, willing her to accept.

"Well, I'm asking her, too," Greg blurted, taking a stance beside Sarita. "Now let go of her."

Sarita barely heard what Greg had said. Her attention was riveted on Wolf. She had never seen such intense purpose on his face and yet she was finding it difficult to believe she'd heard him correctly. "I thought you just wanted to be friends."

He drew her up against him and let the desire she sparked in him show in his eyes. "I don't move as fast as some men. I figured being friends was the way to start. But I'm not going to be undercut by some fancy-talking womanizer."

Greg tried to push them apart. "I'm not some fancy-talking womanizer. I want to marry her." He gave Sarita's shoulder a shake to gain her attention. "Sarita, I know I don't have the best reputation in town, but for you, I'll change."

His touch could not pull her gaze away from the dark, warm depths of Wolf's eyes. Answering passion flamed to life within her.

Wolf read the heat in her eyes, and his need for her grew even stronger. "Marry me." It was an order.

Sarita's rational mind insisted this had to be an illusion. But even in her wildest imaginings she knew she could never have dreamed up the intensity in those brown depths. And the hold on her arm was definitely real.

"Sarita, answer me." Wolf knew he'd stunned her. On the way in, he'd planned a calmer proposal but seeing her with Pike when he'd entered had caused him to snap. All he could think about was getting her away from the man. And now all he could think about was claiming her for his own.

The words to tell him that she needed a minute to think formed on the tip of her tongue, but when she opened her mouth to speak, a single word issued. "When?"

"You can't be serious," Greg snarled.

"Sarita!" Jules and Gladys said in unison, concern mingling with disbelief.

But she didn't hear any of them; she was too intent on Wolf's answer.

"Now," he growled, and began guiding her to the door.

A momentary flicker of reality impinged. "I can't leave Jules in the lurch. The morning rush is just beginning."

Wolf glanced toward Jules. "I'll reimburse you for any losses you suffer because of Sarita's absence."

Jules frowned at him. "I'm not worried about money. But maybe you two shouldn't rush into this. Wait, have a nice wedding here," he coaxed. "I'll do all the cooking for the reception. It'll be fabulous."

It was obvious the man was trying to buy Sarita time to reconsider her actions. That was exactly what Wolf didn't want. "We have an appointment with a minister," he said, and continued guiding Sarita toward the door.

Sarita was aware of the worry on Jules's and Gladys's faces and of Greg cursing under his breath. And, as she and Wolf passed through the dining area, she noticed that there was total silence and the patrons had all left their tables and were gathered near the counter so they could hear what had been happening in the kitchen. But nothing mattered except the feel of Wolf O'Malley's hand wrapped possessively around her arm and the thought that she had agreed to marry him.

"We'll just pack a few things and grab the papers we need," Wolf said as he drove them back to the ranch. "I've reserved the honeymoon suite at one of the best hotels in Phoenix, and Bradford will be waiting for us there. He has a friend who will marry us as soon as we get our license."

Inwardly she experienced a small twinge of embarrassment that she hadn't played a little harder to get. After all, he had been pushing her away for days. "You must have been pretty certain of yourself."

He stroked the line of her jaw, then rested his hand on the back of her neck. "No. Just hopeful and determined. You've always said I was one of the most bull-headed people you know."

The past few days flashed through her mind. "This doesn't seem real."

"It's very real," he assured her.

But how long will it last? her inner voice asked. Everything was happening too fast. Did he really love her or was he doing this just to save her from Greg Pike? He'd been emphatic about keeping her away from the man. Or maybe it was a male ego thing. Maybe there was a long-standing feud between the two men that no one knew about. She told herself that she should call a halt to this until she found out what was the truth. But Wolf was massaging the back of her neck now and all she wanted to do was purr.

To Wolf's relief, Luis was not home when they arrived. Now that he'd chosen this path, he didn't want the old man saying something that might tip Sarita off about the challenge that had been given him and Greg, before he could get her to the altar. Once she was his wife, he would tell her everything and make her see how much he cared for her.

Sarita could barely focus her thoughts on her packing. With every handful, doubts assailed her. She'd never acted on impulse before...well not about something this important. And this was monumental.

"You ready?" Wolf asked from her door.

"I'm not certain what I've packed," she admitted, looking at the contents and wondering if she had the essentials.

"Do you have your birth certificate?"

She held up the piece of paper.

She looked so delectable Wolf's impatience at claiming her for his own grew even stronger. Crossing the room in long strides, he zipped her satchel closed and slung it over his shoulder. "We'll buy anything you've forgotten.'' Giving her fanny a light slap, he added, ''As far as I'm concerned the less the better.''

Fires of desire threatened to consume her. ''I'd better leave my grandfather a note.''

In the kitchen, as she jotted a message to Luis, the argument about whether she should go through with this or call a halt now continued in her mind. Pausing, she asked herself what she really wanted to do. The answer came swiftly—she wanted to marry Wolf O'Malley. She'd never wanted anything so much in her entire life. Signing the note, she firmed her jaw resolutely. She would worry about regrets later; for now, she would go with her instincts. Every one of them told her that she and Wolf belonged together. *Or maybe it's just lust guiding me,* she admitted.

''We need to be going,'' Wolf said, coming up behind her and slipping his arm around her waist.

Her whole body threatened to melt from the heat. She didn't care which was the truth. *Everyone deserves an adventure once in their lifetime,* she told herself. And this could definitely qualify as an adventure. ''I'm ready.''

Again Wolf read the fire in her eyes. All he could think about was getting that marriage license signed. He had never wanted to possess a woman more than he wanted to possess Sarita. His body ached for hers.

Sarita glanced toward the desk in the living room of the fancy hotel suite. There, waiting to be signed, was the marriage license. It had taken a couple of hours to get it, and all that time her insides had been quivering like jelly. She'd been certain that at any moment this fantasy would end. It hadn't.

Now, standing beside Wolf while the Reverend Josh

Jones prepared to guide them through the traditional ceremony, she felt as if she was in a surrealistic play.

Bradford, of course, looked perfect for his role as best man in his three-piece suit. And the reverend was correctly attired, as well as his wife who had come along as the second witness. She was wearing a lovely cotton-print summer dress, perfect for a wedding.

It was only Sarita and Wolf who looked out of place in their blue jeans and shirts. As the minister began the ceremony, a little voice inside Sarita again warned that this was too fast, too unreal. Still she stood beside Wolf reciting her vows.

Suddenly the minister was asking, "Do you, Sarita Carlotta Lopez take Wolf O'Malley to be your lawfully wedded husband? To have and to hold from this day forward, till death do you part?"

This was it. The big question. "I do." The words came out without hesitation.

Her breath locked in her lungs while the minister asked Wolf if he'd take her for his wife. Somewhere from deep inside came a surge of fear that he might suddenly call the whole thing off. He didn't. He made his affirmative response with calm purpose.

As the minister pronounced them man and wife, Wolf breathed a sigh of relief. As for Sarita, her legs suddenly felt as if they were going to crumble.

"And now you may kiss the bride," Reverend Jones instructed.

Wolf took her into his arms, and Sarita suddenly realized she'd married a man she'd never even kissed! Until now a peck on the forehead was the closest they'd come. Then his lips found hers and all thinking ceased. His mouth was warm and inviting. Every sensual fiber in her body began to tingle. She had dreamed about kisses like this, but had thought they only existed in a person's imagination.

Wolf was having a hard time controlling himself. She tasted so good he didn't want to stop until he sampled at least her neck and shoulders. A subtle ''Ahem'' from Bradford reminded him that there were others present. Reluctantly he released his new bride.

Robotlike, Sarita signed all the necessary official documents, then watched Wolf sign, followed by Bradford and the minister's wife.

''All the *i*s are dotted and the *t*s crossed,'' Reverend Jones said, handing the marriage certificate to her. ''How does it feel to be Mrs. Wolf O'Malley?''

''Unreal,'' she replied honestly.

He raised an eyebrow in confusion.

''This calls for a toast,'' Bradford said, saving her from having to provide an explanation for her statement.

As Bradford popped the cork from the bottle of champagne chilling nearby in its silver bucket and poured a round of drinks, Wolf slipped his arm around Sarita's waist and whispered in her ear. ''I plan to make this feel very real, very soon.''

His breath on her neck sent currents of erotic excitement coursing through her. Glancing at him, she saw the passion in his eyes, and the fires within her began to rage once again. Impatience for the others to leave swept through her. *Wanton woman,* she chided herself. But she liked the way she felt. Every part of her being was alive with excitement and anticipation.

Wolf allowed a couple of toasts, then said, ''My bride and I would like to be alone.''

Nothing subtle about that, Sarita thought. But then

Wolf was a man who spoke his mind. He'd also said what was on hers.

Still, as their guests bade them farewell, she became increasingly nervous.

Once alone, Wolf drew her into his embrace. "Sarita Carlotta Lopez O'Malley. I like the sound of that." As he spoke he nibbled on her ear, then trailed kisses along the cord of her neck.

"I do, too." She marveled that anything coherent had come out of her mouth.

Wolf had seen the passion in her eyes. When he felt her muscles tensing he straightened and frowned down at her in confusion. "Is something wrong?"

"I'm just new at this," she said.

"New?"

"Inexperienced." A tiny flush of embarrassment reddened her cheeks, then her shoulders squared with pride. "So, I'm old-fashioned. I saved myself for marriage."

Understanding spread over his face. That he would be her first filled him with a sense of masculine power. "I'm glad."

"That means you're going to have to guide me through this," she added.

"That will be my pleasure." A twinge of nervousness curled through Wolf. He wanted this to be as good for her as it was for him.

"So how do we start?"

"One of us should take something off."

A fresh wave of nervousness swept through Sarita. "Which one?"

He read her uneasiness. "I'll go first." He'd been continuing to hold her loosely in his arms. Now he released her and began unbuttoning his shirt.

"Nice," she said when he finished discarding his shirt and was standing in front of her bare-chested. The word sounded anemic to her ears. "A lot more than nice," she corrected.

For a long moment a silence filled the room. Knowing his patience would only last so long, Wolf broke it. "Would you like some help?"

Sarita drew a tense breath. "My turn, huh?" Her hands went to the buttons of her shirt. As she discarded it, she forced herself to look up into Wolf's face. The approval she saw filled her with womanly pride.

"The boots are definitely uncalled-for," Wolf said. Seating himself in a chair, he discarded his boots and his socks.

"I can see where they could get in the way," Sarita agreed and followed his lead.

"You have more to take off than me. I think you should go next," Wolf instructed when they were both standing facing each other again.

His gaze indicated her bra. Unfastening it, she slipped it off.

"Very nice," he said in a husky growl, cupping her breasts, then kissing the nipple of each.

The urge to scream in ecstasy was almost uncontrollable. Instead, she heard herself saying, "This is going well."

Wolf grinned. "Very well."

She noticed the bulge beneath his jeans and grinned back.

Worried about frightening her when she saw how ready he was, Wolf took the initiative and removed her belt, then began removing her jeans.

"I thought we were going to take turns," she said, playfully reprimanding him.

Wolf was kneeling in front of her and nipped her thigh. "I'm too ready. Now behave and let me do my work."

"Work?" she teased.

She'd stepped out of her jeans, and he was now slowly lowering her panties, letting his fingers follow the curves of her legs as he went. "You have no idea how hard I'm fighting to maintain control."

Fires so hot she thought she might melt were blazing within her. "Maybe I do."

He looked up and saw the passion on her face.

"Time to grasp the moment," he said, slinging her over his shoulder and striding toward the bedroom.

Sarita laughed. "Feels like you grasped more than the moment."

Laughing back, he tossed back the bedcovers, then laid her down. In the next instant he'd shed the rest of his clothes and joined her.

Her body ready, aching for his, Sarita slid into his arms without hesitation.

For one brief moment there was pain, then all was forgotten but the delicious sensations of exotic euphoria as they moved in rhythm, each motion carrying them higher and higher to the peak of ecstasy.

Sarita marveled at the pleasure he was giving her.

Wolf's first reaction to claiming her had been an intensely satisfying sense of possession. Now he was astonished by the way his need to please her continued to grow.

As her climax neared, Sarita began to move more forcefully. Wolf wanted to let out a yell of satisfaction. Then both reached their peaks and all either could do was gasp for breath from the sheer delight of it.

* * *

Sarita awoke the next morning with a sense of fulfillment. Wolf had been all she'd ever hoped for in a sexual partner, and he'd let her know that she had satisfied him, as well. Yesterday still had the feel of a fantasy, but she knew the man lying beside her was very real. Opening her eyes, she looked up from her warm, cozy nest in the crook of his arm.

Wolf's jaw was set in a hard line, and his expression was grim. Something was wrong. Again she wondered if he'd only married her to save her from Greg and that now he realized he was saddled with her for life and regretted his actions.

Wolf felt her head move on his shoulder. He'd been trying to convince himself that he should tell her now about Luis and the canyon. But he was afraid of losing her trust. He would give himself a little more time to convince her of the depth of his feelings. His arm tightened possessively around her and his expression softened into a smile of greeting. "Morning?"

She hated the idea of him pretending to be happy with her. She did not smile back. "You looked like a man with something serious on his mind."

"I was just thinking that Claudia is going to be very disappointed that she missed the wedding. We'll need to make it up to her." This wasn't a total lie. His sister had flickered through his mind while he'd been lying there.

Sarita breathed a mental sigh of relief. She knew Claudia was the only family member Wolf had left to whom he felt close. And she was a teenager. They were the easiest to offend. It was only natural he would worry about upsetting her. "I really don't think you need to worry about Claudia. If you will recall, when I talked to Jules last night to let him know he would need to get someone in to take my place for a few days…"

"There is no reason for you to continue to work at all," Wolf interjected, repeating what he'd said the night before. His hand moved along the curves of her body. "From now on I want you exclusively as my wife."

She rewarded this request with an impatient frown. "I can't leave Jules in the lurch. Like I told you last night, I'll quit as soon as he finds someone permanent to take my place."

"That had better be soon. You're going to have the building of a house to oversee."

He made her feel so very wanted, she thought she was in danger of purring. "And as for Claudia," she continued, wanting to reassure him, "Jules said he'd already called her and asked her to help him plan the reception so that she would feel included. And he said she told him that she thought our elopement was 'hugely romantic.'"

"She's still going to be a little miffed when she finds out Bradford was here." Wolf grinned as if a solution had presented itself. "We'll invite her to the birth of our first child."

"Just what I'm looking forward to," Sarita said dryly. "An audience while I'm in the clutches of labor."

Wolf chuckled. "So maybe we'll think of something else." His stomach growled. "But for now, how about some breakfast." He reached for the room-service menu.

"It was an active night and I am famished," Sarita replied.

"Think I'll have the eggs Benedict and pancakes

with bacon on the side," Wolf said, looking over the menu. "How about the same for you? And a couple of large orange juices and a pot of coffee."

"That's two breakfasts apiece," she pointed out.

He nipped her earlobe. "I'm planning on a very active morning."

Sarita laughed. She'd never been so happy.

Chapter Eleven

Two days later Wolf and Sarita returned to Lost River.

"As soon as the reception Jules and Claudia have planned is over, we're going on a real honeymoon," he promised as they parked in back of the ranch house. "And I'm going to rent us a place of our own until our house is built." He didn't mention that he'd already had Bradford looking for a place for them. The less they were around Luis, the better he would like it.

Sarita recalled that Wolf had been rather cool toward Luis during the couple of days before the elopement. "Did you and my grandfather have an argument?"

"We had a disagreement about how to handle a certain matter."

The grim set of his jaw told her that whatever the disagreement was about, it had been serious. "I know he can be stubborn at times. But so can you." A plea entered her voice. "I hope the two of you will mend your fences. I don't want the two most important men in my life feuding."

Wolf kissed her lightly. Luis, however misguided, had been doing what he thought was best for his granddaughter. Still, Wolf could not entirely bury his anger toward the old man. But he also did not want to deny Sarita anything that would make her happy. "I'll do whatever I can to please you."

Sarita breathed a sigh of relief. "Thanks." Seeing her grandfather coming out of the house to greet them, she climbed out of the car.

Reaching her, Luis gave her a hug. "I would have preferred a church wedding," he said. "But I'll settle for having you married at last."

"Thanks, I think," she replied. The "married at last" part carried the suggestion that he believed she'd crossed the line into spinsterhood.

Releasing her, he clasped Wolf's hand. "I knew the best man would win. My money was on you all the way."

Sarita frowned at her grandfather in confusion. "You knew how Wolf felt about me?"

Luis laughed. "I knew he would not allow you to marry someone as unsuitable as Greg Pike. Wolf is a man of honor."

Sarita experienced an uneasy curl deep within. Her grandfather was suggesting that Wolf had married her to save her from Greg. That had been one of her worries, as well, and hearing it voiced brought it back full force.

Wolf fought to keep his anger in check. The old man had played him like a pawn in a game of chess. That he'd won the queen would have appeased him except that he knew this game could still backfire on him. He wrapped his arm possessively around Sarita's waist. "I married your granddaughter because I love her."

Sarita noted that Wolf's voice rang true, and the curl of uneasiness faded.

Luis nodded with approval. "Come along. I've got some sandwich makings for lunch."

But as Sarita started to follow her grandfather, Wolf caught her arm and held her back. He was normally a man who always forced himself to face the truth. But this was a matter of the heart, and there was a question he had been avoiding asking. He could avoid it no longer. "I've told you why I married you. But you've never actually told me why you married me."

Sarita faced him levelly. "Because you made me so crazy, I knew it had to be love."

Wolf grinned with relief. "Now we can go eat. I'll get our suitcases later." Slipping his arm around her waist once again, he headed toward the house.

Joy bubbled inside of Sarita. She could tell from his expression that her answer had meant a great deal to him. She had definitely made the right decision.

On the kitchen table was a box with a bow.

"My wedding gift," Luis said, nodding toward it.

Curious, Sarita reached for it. "Our first wedding present," she said, smiling up at Wolf. The sudden stiffening of his jaw brought a mental sigh. Obviously whatever he and Luis had argued about was still bothering him so much he was tense about accepting her grandfather's gift. Well, she was determined to make peace between the two men. Opening the box, she found a deed inside. "What's this?"

"It's the deed to the canyon and several acres surrounding it," Luis replied happily.

"I didn't marry your granddaughter for a piece of your land," Wolf growled.

Luis faced him sternly. "It's her dowry."

Wolf glanced at the deed. "Then it should be entirely hers. I want my name removed."

"It is yours and hers. You can do what you want with it," Luis replied.

"I think it's very nice of *Abuelo* to give us such a gift. The canyon will be the perfect place for our horses," Sarita said, trying to make peace.

Wolf drew a terse breath. "All right. But the deed will be changed so that only your name appears on it, just as my mother's name remained on her land."

"If that makes you happy," Sarita conceded, guessing it was pride that was keeping him from accepting the gift for himself. Very soon, she promised herself, she would have a talk with Luis and find out what he and Wolf had argued about, then find some way to settle it between them.

"Let's forget about land and deeds for now and eat," Luis said, waving them to seat themselves.

As he sat down, Wolf knew he couldn't put off telling Sarita about the canyon any longer. But he wanted to do it when they were alone and he could explain that saving her from Greg had only been the catalyst that had made him realize how much he loved her. "As soon as we're finished, we'll take a ride to where I'm thinking of building our house," he said to her. "I want your approval."

"Sounds great," she replied, deciding she would use the opportunity to again try to find out from Wolf what he and her grandfather had fought about. And if Wolf continued to evade her, she would confront Luis. And then she would force the men to confront each other. This very evening, she vowed, she would insist they talk out whatever was between them, before she would allow either to sleep.

They had finished lunch, and Sarita and Luis were putting away the food while Wolf was retrieving the suitcases from the car when there was a knock on the front door.

"I'll see who's here," Wolf said on his way back through the kitchen.

From the front of the house, Sarita heard a youthful voice she recognized as Claudia's. Going out to say hello to her new half sister-in-law, she paused in the hall. Wolf had discarded the suitcases and taken Claudia into the living room. Deciding that he should have a few private moments with his half sister to make amends, she started to pick up the suitcases and carry them on to the bedroom. But what Claudia was saying caught her attention, and her legs refused to move.

"You should have heard Katherine ranting when she found out about your marriage to Sarita. I've never heard her so angry." The teenager's voice was filled with excitement. "It was worth missing your wedding to hear it. Greg Pike was there, and mother was pacing around the study cursing at him. She said she couldn't believe that he had let you win the wager and they'd lost the canyon."

Out in the hall Sarita's stomach knotted into a painful ball.

"This really isn't a good time to be discussing this," Wolf cautioned, glancing toward the door. Mentally he breathed a sigh of relief when he saw no one there.

Like a bubble that had reached the point of bursting and could not stop itself, Claudia merely lowered her voice and continued. "But I found out why Katherine and Greg really wanted the canyon. They wanted it because of this." She thrust a rolled-up piece of rawhide toward him. "Katherine said you might have gotten the land, but you'd never profit by it. She'd been clutching this while she paced. Then suddenly, she went over to the safe and stuck it inside. She didn't know I have the combination. I waited until she was asleep, then sneaked down and took it out." Awe entered Claudia's voice. "It's a treasure map drawn by the Indians. It must be at least a hundred years old and it's of the canyon."

Just beyond the door, Sarita had heard everything. She wanted to run and hide and cry until there were no more tears, but pride refused to allow that. She stepped to the doorway and leveled her gaze on Wolf. "What exactly did Katherine mean about 'winning the wager'?"

Wolf read the pain on her face and hated himself for not having told her the truth sooner. "I was going to explain everything to you when we went riding this afternoon."

Sarita's jaw hardened. "What did she mean?"

Wolf met her gaze. "Your grandfather told Pike he could have the canyon if he married you. I was there and protested. Luis said if I felt that strongly, then I could marry you. And, if either Pike or I told you about the bargain, he'd sell the land to the other."

Out of the corner of her eye, Sarita saw her grandfather in the hall. She turned to glare at him. "How could you?" she demanded.

"It was time for you to have a husband. In my day men married for dowries. I was simply following tradition."

Tears of rage and betrayal threatened to blur her vision.

"I didn't marry you to win a wager," Wolf said, capturing her arm to turn her to him. "I married you because I love you. I didn't tell you about the wager before the marriage for the reason that I didn't want you to lose what was rightly yours because of an old man's stubbornness.''

Claudia had paled as the realization hit her of the damage her exuberance had caused. ''Wolf would never have married you just to win a wager,'' she blurted.

Sarita swallowed back the lump in her throat. ''No. But he would have married me to spite Katherine. I know how deeply his hatred of her runs.''

''If you're thinking that he actually did push her down those stairs, you're wrong,'' Claudia persisted. ''My old nanny was there. She saw the whole thing. Katherine was in a rage because she was all ready to go out and I'd wanted a hug. She'd only meant to get close enough to give me a little peck on the cheek, but I grabbed her hair and mussed it. She was so angry about having to redo her hair, she tripped on her way down the stairs and fell. And that's the truth.''

''I never thought he pushed her down the stairs,'' Sarita said. Unable to face any of them any longer, she jerked free and ran from the house. She had never felt so humiliated or so crushed.

Inside the living room Claudia had burst into tears. ''I'm so sorry,'' she wailed.

Wolf glared at Luis. ''This is all your fault.''

''I did what any grandfather would do. Sarita needed a husband,'' Luis declared. ''Now she is your wife. It is up to you to make things right with her.''

''I intend to,'' Wolf growled. He glanced back at Claudia. ''It'll be all right. I should have told her sooner.''

Cursing Luis under his breath, Wolf strode after Sarita. He was not as confident as he'd sounded, but he was determined. He would do anything to keep her. He caught up with her in the barn. She was saddling her mare.

"Just stay away from me," she warned, the tears that had begun the moment she'd exited the house streaming down her cheeks.

Respecting the warning in her voice, Wolf stopped where he was. "You've got to believe me. I didn't marry you to spite Katherine. I married you because I wanted you for my wife. I want to spend the rest of my life with you."

"I need some time alone. Time to think," she said, cinching the saddle in place. An even more devastating thought occurred to her. "Or maybe you knew about the treasure map. Maybe all of this was for money."

Anger flashed across his face. Closing the distance between them in two long strides, he captured her by the upper arms. "I would never sell my soul or harm the heart of another for money." The hurt her accusation caused showed in his eyes. "You can't really think that of me."

Deep in her soul she knew that accusation had been unfair. Wolf was a difficult man but a good man at heart. "All right. I don't believe you would do that," she admitted. "But your hatred for Katherine runs deep. It could cause you to do things you would not normally do."

Continuing to hold her captive, he leaned closer so that his face was very near hers. "Even the way I feel about Katherine would never have allowed me to bring you any pain."

Frustration raged through her. "I want to believe

you," she confessed. "But your proposal was so sudden. It never did seem really real."

"Don't you think I was astonished by how our relationship changed? All the time we were growing up we were combatants. Then I come back from the dead and there you are...the only one who even cared that I had existed. And I discover I can talk to you and I trust your judgment. It was as though I was seeing you for the first time."

Sarita's chin trembled. She wanted so much to believe him.

Wolf stared hard into her tear-filled eyes. "You know there's a bond between us that can't be broken. It's what caused you to visit my grave site." He drew her up closer to him. "I won't let you run away from me and build a wall between us."

That was exactly what she'd been intending to do...insulate herself so that he could never hurt her again.

"Life for me without you would be empty," he persisted. "Will you really be happy without me?"

She thought about her life without him. It left her feeling hollow. "When I stood by your grave site, I could feel a void inside of me. I didn't understand. We'd never even been friends. But when you came back, it was if the world was complete again," she admitted.

"That's because the two of us together make a whole." Releasing her arms, he cupped her face in his hands. "Please, Sarita. Trust me. Believe in me."

She looked hard into his eyes, seeking any hint of deception. There was none.

"I need you. You wouldn't leave me to face Preston

and Katherine on my own, would you?'' he asked
pleadingly.

A protective urge surged through her. Her mind
flashed back through the past few days—the way he
practically stood guard over her, the frustration she'd
seen on his face when she wouldn't stay away from
Greg, his proposal and her knowing that she really had
no choice but to wed him. And, she confessed silently,
she had no real choice now.... He was her destiny.
Every fiber of her being told her so. ''No. You need
all the help you can get to fend off those two.''

Relief spread over his features. Crushing her to him,
he kissed her...a long, hungry, possessive kiss that
wiped away any fragment of doubt she might have had.

When their lips parted, Wolf continued to stand
holding her to him.

Sarita felt her nose begin to run from all the crying.
''I need a handkerchief,'' she said pushing gently
away.

Releasing her, Wolf produced one from his pocket.

As she blew her nose, Sarita suddenly remembered
Claudia. The teenager had looked totally stricken. ''We
should go inside and assure Claudia that everything is
all right.''

''What about Luis?'' Wolf asked, his anger toward
her grandfather still strong.

Sarita sighed. ''He's an old man. He's not going to
change. But he is my only close relative, and I have
vowed to take care of him in his old age. I'll admit,
I'm angry with him, too, but I can't turn against him.''

Wolf nodded his understanding. ''You're right. And,
in his own way, he did have your best interests at heart.
Guess we'll have to put up with him as he is.''

Sarita smiled gratefully. ''Thanks.''

"Anything to please you," he said, slipping an arm around her shoulders as they headed back inside.

Claudia was sitting on the couch in the living room weeping. Luis was trying to comfort her but to no avail.

"It's all right," Sarita said as she and Wolf entered the room. "The storm has passed and the air is now cleared." She leveled her gaze on her grandfather. "But don't ever try something like that again."

Luis shrugged. "It worked."

"You're incorrigible," she snapped.

He merely shrugged again.

"Are you sure everything is all right?" Claudia demanded, scanning their faces worriedly.

"Yes," Wolf assured her. "You and Jules can get on with the planning of the reception."

From behind them Luis began to chuckle, then he burst into laughter.

Furious that he was finding so much humor in the pain he'd caused, Sarita turned to glare at him and discovered that he'd unrolled the map Claudia had brought and was looking at it. "What's so funny?"

"Take a look." He turned the piece of aged rawhide toward them. "Recognize it?"

Sarita's eyes rounded. "It's my map."

"Yours?" Claudia asked.

Wolf grinned with recognition. "Yes, Sarita's."

Claudia started at Sarita. "Katherine stole it from you?"

"No. Nothing like that. I drew it," Sarita elaborated.

Claudia continued to look confused. "But it's old."

"The rawhide is old, very old," Wolf confirmed. "And the dyes we used were mixed by my great-grandfather on my mother's side. War Eagle was his name. So they are authentic."

Claudia's gaze turned to her brother. "We? I thought you said it was Sarita's map."

"We both drew one and then hid an item where the map indicated the treasure was," Wolf elaborated. "It was a game devised by my great-grandfather. We were to make the maps difficult but not impossible."

"War Eagle thought the competition might bring them together as friends," Luis interjected. "But it only served to strengthen the competitiveness between them."

Claudia's confusion had turned to interest. "And who won?"

"It was a tie," Wolf replied.

"And what were the treasures?" Claudia persisted.

Sarita expected Wolf to say he had forgotten. After all, it had been a long, long time ago. Both had been barely ten. "Mine was a Spanish coin." Reaching into his pocket, Wolf pulled out the old peso Sarita's map had guided him to.

Sarita stared in disbelief. "You still have it?"

He grinned sheepishly. "I've always considered it my good-luck piece."

"And you, Sarita. What was the treasure Wolf hid for you?" Claudia prodded.

Sarita reached into her pocket and pulled out an oval piece of turquoise. "It was this stone." She grinned up at Wolf. "My good-luck piece."

"That is so romantic," Claudia declared.

Sarita continued to smile at Wolf. "Yes, I guess it is."

"I suppose you should have Claudia put this map back where she found it before she gets into trouble," Luis suggested with a wry grin.

As angry as he still was with the old man, Wolf

couldn't keep from grinning back. "Yes, I suppose we should."

"But how did Katherine get it in the first place, I wonder?" Claudia mused.

"Periodically she would have one of her really nasty days and go into my room and find something of mine to throw away...something I'd made or a rock or feather I'd found and kept. I figured if she found the rawhide map, she would claim it was smelling up the house and toss it first chance she got so I asked my father to keep it for me. We boxed it up and stuck it in the back of one of his desk drawers. I'd forgotten about that until now. Katherine must have found it when she went through his things."

Claudia nodded with understanding. "That would explain why it wasn't until after Daddy's death that she got the spa idea into her head."

Drawing Sarita into his arms, Wolf smiled down at her. "You were the real treasure at the end of that map."

As his mouth found hers, Sarita basked in the knowledge that they'd both found the most precious treasure of all—true love.

* * * * *

*Don't miss the exciting adventure
in Elizabeth August's upcoming
Intimate Moments,
LOGAN'S BRIDE,
coming in September 1999.*

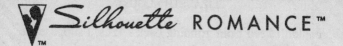

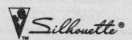

If you enjoyed what you just read,
then we've got an offer you can't resist!

Take 2 bestselling
love stories FREE!

Plus get a FREE surprise gift!

Clip this page and mail it to Silhouette Reader Service™

IN U.S.A.	**IN CANADA**
3010 Walden Ave.	P.O. Box 609
P.O. Box 1867	Fort Erie, Ontario
Buffalo, N.Y. 14240-1867	L2A 5X3

YES! Please send me 2 free Silhouette Romance® novels and my free surprise gift. Then send me 6 brand-new novels every month, which I will receive months before they're available in stores. In the U.S.A., bill me at the bargain price of $2.90 plus 25¢ delivery per book and applicable sales tax, if any*. In Canada, bill me at the bargain price of $3.25 plus 25¢ delivery per book and applicable taxes**. That's the complete price and a savings of over 10% off the cover prices—what a great deal! I understand that accepting the 2 free books and gift places me under no obligation ever to buy any books. I can always return a shipment and cancel at any time. Even if I never buy another book from Silhouette, the 2 free books and gift are mine to keep forever. So why not take us up on our invitation. You'll be glad you did!

215 SEN CNE7
315 SEN CNE9

Name	(PLEASE PRINT)	
Address	Apt.#	
City	State/Prov.	Zip/Postal Code

* Terms and prices subject to change without notice. Sales tax applicable in N.Y.
** Canadian residents will be charged applicable provincial taxes and GST.
   All orders subject to approval. Offer limited to one per household.
   ® are registered trademarks of Harlequin Enterprises Limited.

SROM99   ©1998 Harlequin Enterprises Limited

"Fascinating—you'll want to take
this home!"
—Marie Ferrarella

"Each page is filled with a brand-new
surprise."
—Suzanne Brockmann

"Makes reading a new and joyous
experience all over again."
—Tara Taylor Quinn

See what all your favorite authors
are talking about.

Coming October 1999 to a retail store near you.

THE
FORTUNES
OF TEXAS

*Membership in this family has its privileges...and its price.
But what a fortune can't buy,
a true-bred Texas love is sure to bring!*

Silhouette® brings you a BRAND-NEW program that
includes 12 incredible stories about a wealthy Texas
family rocked by scandal and embedded in mystery. It
is based on the tremendously popular
Fortune's Children continuity.

**Watch for the first book in September 1999
at your favorite retail outlet.**

MILLION DOLLAR MARRIAGE
by Maggie Shayne

**Use this coupon on any Fortunes of Texas title and
receive $1 off.**

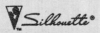

THE
FORTUNES
OF TEXAS

Membership in this family has its privileges...and its price.
But what a fortune can't buy,
a true-bred Texas love is sure to bring!

Silhouette® brings you a BRAND-NEW program that
includes 12 incredible stories about a wealthy Texas
family rocked by scandal and embedded in mystery. It
is based on the tremendously popular
Fortune's Children continuity.

**Watch for the first book in September 1999
at your favorite retail outlet.**

MILLION DOLLAR MARRIAGE
by **Maggie Shayne**

**Use this coupon on any Fortunes of Texas title and
receive $1 off.**

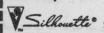

PSFOTUS